pretty like us

CAROL LYNCH WILLIAMS

Ω
PEACHTREE
ATLANTA

Ω
Published by
PEACHTREE PUBLISHERS
1700 Chattahoochee Avenue
Atlanta, Georgia 30318-2112

www.peachtree-online.com

Jacket design by Loraine M. Joyner
Book design by Melanie McMahon Ives

Printed in the United States of America
10 9 8 7 6 5 4 3 2 1
First Edition

Library of Congress Cataloging-in-Publication Data

Williams, Carol Lynch.
  Pretty like us / by Carol Lynch Williams. -- 1st ed.
      p. cm.
  Summary: A shy, small-town girl learns the true meaning of loyalty, love, and beauty
through her friendship with a classmate who is suffering from a rare, life-threatening
illness.
  ISBN 13: 978-1-56145-444-0
  ISBN 10: 1-56145-444-3

  [1. Friendship--Fiction. 2. Progeria--Fiction. 3. Diseases--Fiction.] I. Title.

PZ7.W65588Pr 2008
[Fic]--dc22
                                            2008009858

To Alane Ferguson,
my sister

chapter 1

"**B**eauty," Grandma called from the kitchen. "Quit staring at yourself and get on down here to breakfast."

"I'm not staring at myself," I hollered back. "I'm getting ready for school."

Don't think about school, I whispered. *Just get ready and don't think about it.*

I leaned closer to the mirror and applied a bit more mascara. I'd sneaked a tube off Momma's dresser on account of it being the first day of sixth grade. I already had a couple of strikes against me, and light-colored eyelashes didn't need to be another.

Momma called up the stairs next. "Baby, you gotta hurry yourself on down here. Breakfast is getting cold. You do wanna eat, don't you?"

"You can do this, Beauty," I told my reflection. I blinked into the mirror. The mascara made it look like spiders were crawling around my eyeballs. I don't ever wear makeup. But today was going to be different. It *had* to be.

I needed a song to spur me on. I write songs all the time for special occasions like this. The words usually come to me with no trouble, but to make things simpler I always use the tune to "On Top of Old Smoky."

It is Wednesday morning,
The first day of school.
I'll meet all my good friends...

I couldn't finish. My knees went weak for a second, and I let the sink hold me up.

"Don't think of what's coming, Miss Pretty Is," I said to the mirror.

Now I sounded just like Grandma. "Pretty is as pretty diz," she always says. It's our family motto, Great-Granny Dorothy Lu Lu's version of "Pretty is as pretty does." And according to my mother and grandmother, I am the spitting image of my great-grandmother, right down to the light-colored eyelashes and the shyness gene.

The yummy smell of breakfast made its way into our bathroom. Momma wants to open her own restaurant here in Green River some day. And she can, she's such a great cook. But on this particular morning, biscuit smells and nerves mixed around in my tummy, making me feel queasy.

Reaching around under the sink, I found the hair dryer. I turned it on and waved it in front of the door, trying to blow the odors out into the hall.

When I turned back to the mirror, I noticed that the mascara had smeared. "Great. Just great," I said. "I can't even put mascara on right." I'd jabbed myself in the eyeball twice already and now this. I put down the hair dryer and grabbed a Q-tip. The dryer blew hot air into the daisy shower curtain. It billowed inwards, exposing the claw feet on the bathtub. I managed to clean off most of the smudges under my eyes. I had to Be Perfect today. I had to Do Better this year.

If I could make just one good friend, I thought, *that will be enough to get me through sixth grade.*

Wait. Make a friend? Not be afraid? Not be shy?

That was a joke. Forget doing anything different with my hair or my eyelashes. Or even wearing the new clothes I picked out just for today. A wave of despair washed over me.

I turned off the hair dryer and started downstairs, one slow step at a time.

"Beauty?" Grandma said. "Hurry in here."

Hearing her call out my name again made me cringe. I have plenty of other problems, but my biggest disadvantage in the whole wide world is my name. I mean to say, I am not Beauty from *Beauty and the Beast,* and my life is not a fairy tale. But sure enough, my name is Beauty McElwrath.

The aroma of biscuits and sausage gravy and coffee met me

3

at the bottom of the stairs. "Just a sec," I said as I turned toward the front door instead of the kitchen. Maybe a little morning air would settle my stomach and give me the courage to go to school.

My only friend *had* been Cody Nelson. He didn't seem to care about my name at all. Things between us had been fine. Then he saw I was getting bosoms and that was the last of him.

"Beauty, y-you're..." he'd said, staring right at my chest. "You, know, getting...stuff."

I'd said, "Yeah, so what?" and crossed my arms. It's not like his announcement was news to me. *I'd* noticed already.

Then he'd said, "I didn't think..."

Then I'd said, "You didn't think what? That I'm a girl?"

Then he'd said, "I gotta go."

That was at the beginning of summer, almost three months ago, and we hadn't done a thing together since.

As if I could help the bosoms, or stop them from appearing. As if I even wanted them.

I stood looking out through the lace curtain that covers the glass of our front door. All I could see through the white threads was a fuzzy pattern of trees and yard and driveway.

Things were going to be the way they'd always been, I just knew it. Me all alone with my silly name, watching people from the sidelines. And our family motto wouldn't help me any, either. I might be pretty, like Momma and Grandma always said. And I might act good and kind, like they said I should.

But none of that gave me friends, which made school awful lonely.

A big ol' glob of sadness made tears come to my eyes, but I didn't let myself cry. I didn't want to face Momma and Grandma with black streaks running down my face. I swallowed, then made my way back to the kitchen without getting even one breath of air.

Flash!

"Got you!" Grandma said, waving a camera. "I was wondering if you'd ever make it down here. Give me a hug." She held her arms out and I walked straight into them. She smelled of morning yard work.

"Geez, Grandma," I said. "You're choking the life out of me." I squinched my eyes closed and watched the greenish-colored dots drifting out into the space behind my eyelids. This was where I belonged. Right here in the kitchen with my family. I kissed Grandma's face and padded over to the stove where Momma stood in her blue Dickie's Gas and Other Services coveralls. "Morning," I said.

Momma turned around. "You," she said pointing with a greasy metal spatula, "are as pretty as a new dawn. Mommy, did you get a good shot of these sparkling eyes? Eyes with mascara on them." Momma let out a whistle and I ducked my head.

"Yes, sir, I sure did." Grandma kept snapping photos left and right, pushing her long hair over her shoulder so it wouldn't get in front of the lens.

The three of us McElwraths look a lot alike. Same thick honey-colored hair, same blue eyes, same dash of freckles across the nose. In fact, once when the three of us were standing in line at the WalMart cash register, the clerk asked if we were sisters. But we differ in one important area: My momma and my grandma can talk to anybody in the whole world and it doesn't scare them a bit. Momma was even on the six o'clock news one time—being interviewed by a TV crew about a seven-foot rattlesnake she shot out back of Dickie's Gas and Other Services. And she wasn't nervous at all.

But me? Tell me to ask someone directions to the Flying Burger in Cocoa Beach or inform the librarian that we're sorry our books are two weeks late and I can feel my heart hammering right behind my nostrils. And sweat? I swear, I can feel the sweat right now just thinking about it.

Whoever heard of being like that at the age of twelve?

"Turn around so I can see all of you," Momma said, swirling her spatula in the air.

"Yes, ma'am." I tried to sound grumpy, but I couldn't. Instead, I spun in my new faded blue jeans and pink top with the glitter heart that Momma and I bought with Grandma's extra discount from working as a cashier at the Shop-For-Less.

Pop! Pop! Pop! went the camera again.

"That should about do it," Grandma said at last. "Thirty-six photos of my grandbaby's first day in sixth grade. These are going to be great."

"Sit down, Beauty, so I can feed you," Momma said, smashing a kiss into my temple. She set a plate of cheesy biscuits and a pan of sausage gravy on the yellow gingham tablecloth. As she poured orange juice in my cup, a patch of sunshine landed on the glass pitcher, making it look like a sunrise. "Now fill up that plate and eat, Baby, so you can learn all there is to learn today."

I sat down and said a little prayer in my heart. *Beauty, you're as ready as you'll ever be. This year you're going to do it. You're going to find yourself a true friend.*

And in spite of the shaking in my knees and the way my left eye kept twitching, I believed every word.

chapter 2

I made Momma hide behind the old oak at the front of our property, the one whose limbs sweep down so low I use them as steps to climb into the branches. I suggested that she go up at least partway so she'd be completely out of sight, but Momma said, "Beauty, it's bad enough you're embarrassed of me. I am *not* going up with the jays."

So I didn't press my luck.

"I am not embarrassed of you," I said, throwing my voice over my shoulder so she could hear me. It would be the death of my sixth-grade social life if anyone saw my momma standing out at the bus stop with me. Last year I cried when she dropped me off at school, and half the kids in my class had seen me clinging to her. They'd teased me forever.

I looked down the road for the bus full of kids that would be coming any minute. My lips were trembling and my hands were so sweaty I could have watered the front lawn.

"Are you okay?" Momma asked. She peered between the leaves.

"Don't show your face where someone might see it," I said, flapping my hands to shoo her to her hiding place.

She tucked her head in behind the oak. "Baby, you don't need me here."

"I do. I do." I wanted to run back and squeeze her neck hard in a hug. But instead I stared out at the dark green of the woods on the far side of our property. The ground under the trees was bare of grass, because only a tiny bit of sun can get through.

I gulped hard. I thought maybe I could taste breakfast all over again.

"You're not going to throw up, are you?" Momma gave a little laugh. She always laughs at stuff like that. Sometimes I think I am the most mature person in the McElwrath household.

"Of course not," I said. "I haven't puked from nerves in a forever."

"Ha," Momma said. "You puked on Space Mountain no more than two months ago."

"That," I said, "does not count. Fast movements get to me."

"I know, Baby," Momma said. "I was just kidding. Face forward on the bus, and you'll be fine."

We were quiet. So quiet I could hear the breeze in the top of the oak tree and the chatter of early morning squirrels and birds. But no bus sounds. Where the heck was it, anyway? I wanted to get this whole thing over with.

"It'll be better this year," Momma said. "I promise, Beauty. I got the best feeling that things are gonna go great for you."

Quick tears stung my eyes. Momma knows me inside and out. Boy, do I love her.

"You got a real decent chance that Jamie is gonna be your teacher," she said. "That's good, isn't it?"

It felt like my heart squeezed to a stop. "Momma? Tell me you didn't. Tell me you didn't do anything—"

"I'm going now," she said. And just like that, she took off at a jog, heading toward the house, her hair flying out behind her.

Oh...no.

Now I had something else to worry about.

I watched Momma run all the way down our long driveway. I wanted to follow her, run past her even, back home. Maybe I could get a job helping her at Dickie's Gas and Other Services, handing her tools or something. I didn't need to go to school.

But I didn't run home. Instead, I stood in the Florida sun and hoped for Momma to be right about the year being good, but wrong about Jamie being my teacher. Then I saw the bus down the road, and my heart thumped. The bus stopped in front of me, the doors opening with a *whoosh*.

I climbed the steps and looked for Cody.

He wasn't there.

Good, I thought. *He wouldn't have talked to me anyway.* I flopped down in an empty seat, too much of a scaredy cat to look for someone to sit with in this big vehicle full of kids.

✳

"Well, hello, Beauty McElwrath," Jamie Borget said when I got to my classroom door. "Guess whose class you're in."

Of course, he knew I knew, because I had picked up my class assignment in the cafeteria as soon as I walked into the school. But I decided to go along. I took in a deep breath to settle myself. "Yours?"

He grinned at me. "Yes, you are right."

"Jamie," I said, "Momma wasn't supposed to mess with anything. She was supposed to..." I looked down at my shoes and kicked at a sandy footprint on the used-to-be clean turquoise floor.

"This was the luck of the draw," he said. "I had very little to do with you winding up in here." Then he lowered his voice. "Just remember to call me *Mr. Borget* as long as we're in school. Okay?" He winked at me.

"Great," I said.

"Try it again."

"Great," I said. Only this time I made my voice all singsong. It was weird seeing him all dressed up, wearing a tie and everything.

11

He laughed. "No, try my teacher name again."

This was not going to be easy. All summer Mr. Borget had insisted I call him Jamie. *Now* he wanted a change? On this most important, most frightening day of my life? Wasn't it bad enough that my mother's new boyfriend was going to be my teacher for nine long months? Why couldn't he just pretend not to know me?

"Good morning, Mister Borget," I said.

"Good to see you, Beauty," he said. "Go find a seat."

I lingered outside the door for a minute, looking over the room assignments posted on the wall. Cody was in this class, too. That made my heart pound good and hard. Sweat eased its way down my back and a sharp pain stabbed behind my right eye.

There are only two sixth-grade classes at Green River School for Kindergarten through Sixth Grade: Mine with Jamie—I mean Mr. Borget—and one across the hall taught by Mrs. Simmons, who is not related to that old guy on Grandma's exercise video.

Jamie was a tough teacher. I'd already heard, straight from his mouth, that he makes you do all your homework. And obey a whole bunch of rules. And stretch your mind like a rubber band.

I knew all this because Momma and Jamie had been dating each other for the last four and a half months. He'd come to our house lots of times, but he'd never worn a tie. Nope, at our place he was always casual. Barefoot on hot afternoons down by the river. Happy in the evenings when he took Momma to the movies. Laughing when we visited Disney. He and Momma were good friends, like me and Cody used to be. Before the you-know-whats showed up.

I went in to find a seat. A little left of front and center, I saw a chair with masking tape draped across it, like it was reserved for someone. That seemed weird, but I plopped down in the chair next to it anyway. This year I wasn't hiding in my usual spot back by the bookshelves. This year things were going to be different.

I heard chatter and laughing in the hall, and then Cody came in the room with three other guys.

"Hey, Beauty," he said as he walked past.

"Oh," I said, folding my arms across my chest.

He and the other boys went on to the back of the room.

I put my head down on my desk. You'd think I'd be able to say more than "Oh" to my used-to-be best friend. I'd told him every single one of my secrets out on the edge of the river not that long ago. And he'd told me his, too, like about how his momma and daddy won't even speak to each other but they keep having babies.

Cody was the person, I had been sure before my bosomly attributes appeared, that I would marry. Of course, I never informed him of this. As far as I was concerned, it was none of his business.

"Good morning, class," Mr. Borget said after the first bell rang. He called the roll, and my name got the usual amount of snickers. He pressed on until he got to Dolly Zeiler, then closed the roll book. "I don't know how many of you noticed that we have an empty seat here." He motioned at the desk with the tape on it.

I nodded. *I* had noticed, of course. Noticing things is one of my strong points. It helps in my songwriting. I'll have you know right now that I take a lot of pride in my songs, even if no one but Momma and Grandma will ever hear a single one of them. I'd be too scared to ever perform in public.

A song started up in my mind as I stared at the desk... *In the front of the classroom, one bare empty seat...* I almost hummed out loud.

"We're getting a...a new student this afternoon." Mr. Borget gazed out the window to the playground, where an old magnolia stood, and further off, to the fence that separates us from Green River.

Now, I have to tell you something that I like about this guy. He's never at a loss for words. He's got a mouth full of them. So it was kind of strange listening to him stumble around looking for the right one.

The class of twenty-five kids turned silent. I could hear the buzz of the fluorescent lights above.

"She's moved here from Oklahoma. And..." He looked back at us and rubbed his hand through his hair like he does when

Momma's beating him at Scrabble and he's trying to come up with a great word. "And she has a...disease."

Everyone came alive then. "Like, AIDS?" the boy behind me said. "I bet it's cancer," someone else whispered. Chalice Brown turned to her best friend Maria Keats. "I hope we can't get it," she said, and Maria nodded.

I had chosen the seat next to the sick person without even knowing it.

Our teacher raised his hands to quiet everyone. "She has progeria," he said, "and it's not contagious. It's an aging disorder. Her mother and father wanted me to let you know ahead of time that she looks...well, different."

"How?"

That was Cody. I'd know his voice anywhere. I peeked over my shoulder. He sat next to Ryan Harding.

"Yeah," said Ryan. "What's wrong with the way she looks?"

Mr. Borget cleared his throat. "She has an affliction that makes her age faster. Her body is..." And there he was, stammering again. This had to be something really bad. The last time I saw that expression on his face was after the main character died in this old Italian movie he and my mom watched at our house. For a second, I thought he was gonna bawl, like he did during the video. For sure I wasn't going to laugh at my teacher the way I had that night. This time, there was no kitchen pantry to hide in.

15

But thank the good Lord, he didn't. Instead, he smiled at us. "Be kind, everyone," he said, glancing around the room. Then he stared right at me. "Don't let appearances make you shy or mean. Be kind."

For a moment it felt like we were back in my living room, him telling me that reading is the coolest thing this side of Mountain Dew Icees. Or saying how gazing at the night sky fills a body with wonderment. Or explaining that snakes are the most interesting of the reptiles because of their salivary glands. That's how he stared at me right at that moment. Like no one was around. Like he wanted *me* to know this thing more than he wanted anyone else to know it. It was embarrassing. I looked away.

"What's the new person's name?" Maria asked. She's the one who made fun of me last year because of my clothes. I guess I need to come straight out with it and say that we McElwraths don't have a lot of money. A little bit of land—three acres on the river—our old house, and each other: That's about the extent of our richness.

So you can put down "pretty darn poor" as my second biggest disadvantage. No one else has given me grief about being poor, but just about everyone who has heard my name— not including Cody—has teased me about it for two whole years. As if my name's my fault. As if I wanted such a Look-at-Me name. I've heard enough how'd-you-ever-get-a-name-like-that? comments to last me two lifetimes.

"Her name is Alane Shriver."

Why did he keep looking straight at me? It made me even more nervous than I already was. He still had that funny look on his face. And I saw, somehow, that I was tied up in it.

chapter 3

Here's what we'll do," Maria said. She and two other girls, Dolly and Chalice, sat together at the other end of the lunch table.

You see, I'm not only a noticer, but I'm also a listener. I have no trouble eavesdropping on other people's conversations, even from this far away. "We'll have a party for her at my house," Maria said. "You know, to welcome her."

I peeked into my lunch bag. There it was. A lunch fit for a fancy restaurant—sweetened cream cheese (fruit added) on homemade wheat and walnut bread, fresh-cut pineapple, and a big ol' caramel brownie.

Momma's voice came into my head. "Beauty, when you see this lunch, I want you to have the strength to speak up. Don't be shy. Remember that you are a beautiful girl. You can talk to anyone you want."

I let out a sigh and took a bite of the brownie.

"A party?" Dolly said. She had the school lunch: tacos with refried beans and smelly red rice. Dolly is as short as I am tall. "We don't even know her, Maria. Maybe she won't *want* to come."

"Yeah," said Chalice. "She might be a loser, along with having a disease." Chalice looked right at me. She caught me staring and everything.

I tried to look like I didn't care.

"We don't need to be around any more geeks than we have to," Chalice said.

I quick-looked away from the three of them, but I couldn't stop the hot blush I felt creeping up my neck and face.

"Keep it down," Maria said. "Do you want us to have to ask *her*, too?"

Chalice laughed. They moved closer together. I had to strain to hear what they were saying now, what with all the lunchroom noise.

"Everyone wants to be friends with us," Maria said. "Don't worry. The new girl will come to our party if we ask her."

I pretended to stare out the window at a basketball game in progress on the playground. I couldn't help it. I wanted to go to their party. An ache started up in my throat. What I wanted was to go home.

Maria leaned across the table to Dolly and Chalice. "We'll have to be nice to the new girl. Can you imagine having a disease?"

"I had warts once," Dolly said.

"Gross," Chalice said.

"One was so bad,"—Dolly didn't even pause—"that the doctor thought it might be cancer. He showed my father a big fat book full of disgusting pictures, and he nearly fainted from the sight of them."

"Who? The doctor?"

"No, my dad."

"Shut up, right this second," Chalice said. With my left eye I could see that she looked a little green around the gills. She pushed her tray back.

"So?" Maria said.

"So what?" Dolly said.

"So was it cancer?"

Dolly shook her head and her long red hair swung back and forth. "Nope, just a wart."

"It is our duty," Maria said, "to befriend those in need. Like we took in Dolly here. *She* didn't have friends until we let her hang out with us. It is our duty to be kind to everyone."

She didn't even look in my direction.

*

I went back to the classroom fast as I could. No need to sit alone in the lunchroom with everybody *seeing* me alone.

The room wasn't empty. Mr. Borget sat at my desk, talking

with a tiny old woman. They'd spread their lunches out on the desktops. I wondered if she was somebody's grandma visiting about her grandkid the very first day. Ooo-eee, somebody was gonna be embarrassed as heck finding this out.

"Oh hi, Beauty," Mr. Borget said, smiling and waving me over. I felt relief at hearing his voice, like I was home and safe.

The old lady looked at me, a carton of milk to her lips. She smiled, too.

"Beauty, come here and meet Alane Shriver, our brand new student."

I couldn't move. I wanted to say, "That's not a kid." I wanted to say, "Look here, Jamie, this person is older than my great-granny Dorothy Lu Lu, who's dead." I wanted to ask him, "Can't you see how wrinkled her skin is?" But my tongue just sat there in my mouth.

My legs wouldn't work, either. I stood so still I could hear the crunch when Alane bit into a chip. My eyes had taken control. They wouldn't stop staring right at Alane.

"Alane, Beauty," Mr. Borget said. "Beauty, Alane."

"Beauty?" Alane said. "That's your real name?"

I nodded. In slow motion I started across the classroom floor, as if my eyes were pulling me in closer for a better look. She was so small. And shriveled. Like fruit left outside. Like she was seventy years old.

"How cool," Alane said. "My name means almost the same thing, 'fair one' or 'beautiful.'"

21

I tugged at my shirt, stretching it down the way Grandma always tells me not to. *Her? Beautiful?* If anyone in our class found out what Alane's name meant, well, she was done for. They would sacrifice her to the teasing god without a second thought. "That's great," I said.

I heard him wrong, I thought. *He must have said this is Alane's grandma.*

Now I was close enough to see her hands. They were tiny, like her whole self—small and frail—except for the knuckles. Those were knobby and swollen looking. And her fingers were all crooked, like they had lost their way growing.

I wiped my own damp hands on my blue jeans.

The hall intercom buzzed and a voice called for Ms. Haddon, our principal.

Alane wore a pair of gold glasses that made her eyes look way too big.

"It's nice to meet you," she said. Her voice was high and thin, like she'd sucked helium right before she started talking.

"Sure," I said. "I mean, you too." My voice, thank the good Lord, came out sounding all right this time. Not like I was shocked to death.

We looked at each other and then Alane gave me another smile, a slow one that showed the braces on her teeth. *This is me,* she seemed to be saying, *Are you okay with it?*

No, I wasn't okay with it at all.

I kept staring.

The braces seemed wrong. Like when you see an older person in them and you think, why get them now? Everything about her was just plain weird. I'd been in here two minutes—though it seemed longer—and I needed to leave.

"I came in for...um...a volleyball," I said. The moment the lie left my mouth, I could hear Grandma's voice as clear as stream water: *Pretty is as pretty diz, Beauty.*

"Ten minutes left for lunch," Mr. Borget said. "No time for that." He waved his hand around the room. "Why don't you join us? We're just getting acquainted here."

I tugged at my shirt again. I had to think of a good excuse quick, or else I'd be caught in here with my teacher and...and the disease girl. "Why don't you come outside with me, Alane?" I said, staring off over her shoulder, out the window. "I could introduce you around."

"No, thank you, I don't think so." Alane ran a hand through her long dark hair—the only pretty thing I could see on her body. "I've got to finish my lunch and clean up before everyone comes in."

I looked her in the eye then. She was giving me a way out. This strange little woman-girl was being nice. To me. The person who couldn't live up to her own family motto.

I tucked the volleyball under my arm and hurried out of the room.

chapter 4

I slammed out of the building. The sun, full of September, was blazing overhead. As I ran across the playground a plan popped into my head. I'm not sure where it came from. And I don't know what made me think on it longer than a second. Maybe it was my worry of loneliness. Or fear. I knew for sure that it wasn't something my mother or my grandmother—or any McElwrath for all the generations of time—would have liked. It was not a pretty-is plan. But I didn't turn back.

I ran toward the big magnolia tree, where Cody, Ryan, Maria, Dolly, and Chalice stood in the shade.

"I've seen her," I said when I got closer.

"Who?" Ryan said.

"The new girl." I felt the meanness rising in my throat.

"You did?" Chalice leaned toward me, the way she used to in third grade when we were all equals. "The sick one?"

"Who else would she be talking about?" Maria said. She pushed Chalice aside and looked at me. "And?"

I shook my head. I could practically hear the voices screeching at me, Momma saying, "Don't you do it," and Grandma starting the Pretty-Is lecture. But I ignored them.

"I've never seen anything like her," I said, panting from my sprint across the playground.

Cody looked at the school like he expected the new girl to come outside. "What do you mean?"

Those words, besides the quick greeting in class that morning, were all Cody had spoken to me in months.

I felt homesick again. I didn't want to be here at school another minute. I wanted to be sitting at the edge of the river. I wanted to be away from my own mean self.

"Come on, Beauty," Maria said, wiggling give-me-more fingers. "Tell us."

"She didn't see anyone," Dolly said.

"Shut up, Dolly," Maria and Chalice said at the same time. Then Chalice said, "I want to know what Beauty saw."

I looked at Cody. Then I looked at Ryan and Chalice and Maria and Dolly and thought about being all alone for another school year.

"I did," I said. "Swear. And she's really old."

"What do you mean, old?" Chalice asked. She twisted her brown braid like she was nervous or something. "Like, in junior high?"

"Go on." Maria sounded eager.

Maybe, maybe, this would put me in with them. Maybe they would like me better after I told all I knew. "There's something bad wrong with her." I kept my voice low, so they'd have to come in close to hear.

We all moved into a huddle. The thing I had hoped for was happening at last. People were listening to *me*. *I* was hanging with the cute guys and the popular girls. I hoped I wouldn't choke on the lump in my throat. "She's all...old," I whispered, "like a dried-up apple."

"An apple?" said Dolly.

"Shhh," said Maria. She held up her hand like she was slowing traffic. Her nails were painted pale purple to match her shirt.

"Let Beauty talk," said Chalice.

Ryan moved closer. Cody, too.

I took a deep breath. "I walked in our classroom and I thought someone's *grand*mother had come for a visit."

"But she's supposed to be our age," Cody said. "That's why she's in our class."

"I know. But she looks seventy. Or a hundred. Whatever. Just not our age. She's small, too. It's like she never grew past third grade or something."

"So she's a freakoid," Ryan said.

I nodded.

"That is so sad," Dolly said. "But I don't get it. How can she be that way?"

"It's like Mr. Borget told us," Chalice said. "She has an aging disease."

"Her hands are all twisted." My mouth wouldn't stop. Me, the girl who couldn't say anything to anyone, couldn't stop talking now. "She's sort of bent over and she has braces on her teeth." The more I talked, the weirder I felt. My heart felt flat and mushy, like a balloon with a slow leak. But maybe, finally, things would change for me now.

I wasn't the freakoid anymore.

"She sounds scary," Dolly said.

Chalice got this determined-looking expression on her face. "Well, then. We'll just have to stay away from this girl."

"No party, for absolute sure," Maria said.

The bell rang.

"Thanks for telling us, Beauty," Chalice said. Then they all turned and hurried toward the building. Even Cody.

Be careful now, I told myself. I felt like a baby might, taking her first steps. I stayed behind them a little, on the outside. Then Chalice turned around, and right there in front of Cody said, "Beauty, why are you following us?"

Those words stopped me like a slap. I couldn't even open my mouth to speak. My face burned hot as fire.

"Forget it," Ryan said. "Let's just go see the freak."

27

"Beauty McElwrath says the new girl's ugly, like a prune," Maria said to another kid who came up beside them.

Cody looked at me. "See you later, Beauty," he said. He held my gaze a moment, then walked on. In just a couple of minutes, the playground was empty.

I was alone. Again. Standing there in the sun, smelling the freshly cut first-day-of-school grass and hearing the bell sound a second time, saying I was late.

Everything about me seemed to sag, and I thought I might just plop onto the ground and never get up. Had I really thought that being mean to someone else would make those kids like me? And why hadn't I noticed that Cody was just like them?

I looked at the wide-open double doors that led into the school. I could hear voices sounding from down the hall. Kids laughing. I could smell leftover tacos from the cafeteria. I could imagine the shock everyone was getting, right about now, as they walked into class and saw her there. Alane Shriver, old woman playing sixth grader.

It seemed like I stood there hours without moving, almost in the building, almost out of it. Then I turned and hightailed it off school property as fast as I could.

Straight to Momma at Dickie's Gas and Other Services.

chapter 5

omma saw me coming from down the block. I know 'cause I saw her put both fists on her hips and cock her head to one side. She just stood there, waiting, her hair shining in the sun.

For a second I thought of just running on home. But home seemed too far away right then, and I needed Momma bad. Besides, she'd seen me already.

"Beauty McElwrath, what in the world?" Momma called as soon as we were within shouting distance of each other.

I didn't answer.

"What are you doing out of school, young lady?" Her voice echoed down the street toward me. "And it's only the first day."

Two old men sitting in front of the barbershop stared at me. I waved. The guy in the plaid shirt waved back.

"Hold on, Momma!" I hollered. Did all of Green River need to know what was going on in my life?

When I passed in front of the Green River Soda Fountain and Drug Store, Mrs. Cromwell—who I used to think was the oldest-looking person in the world until I saw Alane—said through the dusty screen door, "School out early, Beauty girl?"

"Just for me," I said. No need to speak up because she couldn't hear me anyway. Or anyone else for that matter. If I could've taken a few minutes, I would've walked right in, climbed up on a shiny yellow counter stool, and had her make me a Coke with three squirts extra vanilla.

But Momma was waiting. And Momma means trouble when she has her hands planted on her hips like she's keeping herself firm on the ground.

"Now listen," I said when I was close enough to see Momma's face better. Her lips, drawn in a tight, thin line, caused my eyes to tear right up.

If anyone tells you most mothers do not have eyes like a hawk, don't believe them. *My* mother does, and Grandma, too. Grandma says Great-Granny Dorothy Lu Lu did before her, and so on and so on and so on. Hawk-eye sight is a motherly trait, like rabbit-ear hearing, or the power to sense what someone is doing in the next room.

Soon as Momma saw my first glimmer of tears, she leapt, and I do mean leapt, across the street to me. It's a good thing that the red light worked in her favor, because she didn't even look to the left or the right. She just ran across to me, grabbed me tight in her arms, and squeezed the air from my lungs in a hug. "Baby girl, what is the matter?" she said over and over. "Tell me. Tell me everything."

And right there across the street from Dickie's place, holding on to my mother in her dirty blue coveralls, I started bawling. I couldn't answer her right away. First off, Momma did have a tight grip on me. And second, I felt rotten inside. Horrible and disgusting and hateful and everything else a person should *not* feel on her first day of sixth grade. So instead of talking, I cried.

Momma called across the street, "Dickie, I'm taking me a break."

I peeked under Momma's arm. Dickie and his son Rickie stood beside the gas pumps in coveralls the same as Momma wore, watching us like we were in a movie or something.

"What happened, Beauty?" Momma said. "Are you hurt?"

"Ye-e-e-e-s." This came out a wail. And with it I felt the loneliness I'd had in class, at lunch, and all day crash down on me again. Even worse than that, I felt the guilt. For gossiping about Alane. For leaving her all alone.

Standing there on the corner of First and Main, cars sweeping past us at thirty-five miles an hour, and the sun shining down like there wasn't a problem in anybody's world, I realized I had destroyed the family motto. I hadn't been pretty *anything* today. In the few seconds Momma and I stood there all smushed together, I started thinking maybe, just maybe, Alane felt worse than I did right at this minute. And maybe, just maybe, I could have been there for her.

31

But I'd been scared.

And I was scareder still to tell Momma the truth of it.

With one arm around my waist, she guided me down the sidewalk, back toward Green River Soda Fountain and Drug Store.

"A vanilla Coke will do you good."

Snuffling, I nodded.

"And you can tell me everything."

Another sob welled up in the back of my throat, but I swallowed it down.

"I tell you," Momma said, her hand tightening at my waist a little more as she talked, "I have half a mind to head right over there to that school and raise some Cain. Were they teasing you about your name again?" Momma shook her head. "Or did you have to talk in class? I told Jamie to give you some time. I mean, he has to remember how long it was before you were comfortable even speaking with him..."

Momma said a few other things, I think, but I burst forth with another wail that drowned her out.

I could feel her body trembling. She was that mad. "Is this my fault, Beauty? Just because I was fourteen when you were born doesn't mean the world has to treat you different." She pushed us both into the drugstore, where Mrs. Cromwell started our order without even asking what we wanted.

I checked myself out in the mirror above the soda fountain. Oh, did I look bad. I mean *bad*. My eyes were squinched up in two tight lines and my face was all red and puffy, the fancy mascara running down my cheeks. I'd worked so hard to look just right. And I'd had such high hopes. Hopes I'd managed to destroy by doing what I'd aimed to do: getting other people to listen to me.

Momma fumed on until Mrs. Cromwell set our drinks and a fresh order of hot fries with two paper cups of spicy dipping sauce in front of us. "Okay, Baby. Tell all. Spill your guts. I am here for you."

I told the story from the beginning, from me sitting all alone on the bus to being nervous about having Jamie as my teacher to meeting Alane Shriver. When I got to the part where I'd said all those mean things to the others about Alane, Momma froze, a french fry almost to her lips. Then she set it down, spicy sauce and all, on the edge of our shared plate. The salt on the potatoes sparkled like tiny diamonds.

Mrs. Cromwell looked up, like maybe she'd heard what I said. Even Mr. Cromwell peered out at us from behind the glass of the pharmacy section.

"You did what?" Momma's voice was low, but it had the energy of a Florida hurricane behind it. "You...did...what?"

"I don't know what I was thinking." The smell of grilling hamburgers, cracked pepper, and onions floated in the air. Someone at a back booth coughed. Had they heard, too?

"You...weren't...thinking...at all," Momma said, the words slower than I could have finger-spelled them.

"I know, I know." I clutched the cold glass of Coke with both hands. Something like a fever rode up from my chest, crept onto my neck, and heated up my face.

"You know our family motto. You *know* we treat people good, no matter what. And Beauty, you of all people should know why we do that."

I nodded. "Because of how bad it feels when someone is mean to us."

Momma slumped forward on her stool, leaning her elbows on the shiny countertop. "So why?" she asked. "Why did you do it, Beauty?"

The tears came again. "I thought if I told those kids stuff, they'd let me be friends with them."

Momma was quiet a moment. "And they didn't," she said, letting a sigh escape with the words.

"They didn't," I said, feeling almost black inside.

"But for a little bit,"—Momma took in a deep breath through her nose—"you acted just like them. Though I must admit that I'm surprised at Cody acting that way."

Cody? She didn't know a thing about him.

"And you, too, Beauty."

Her next words poked me in the chest.

"Was it worth it?"

I shook my head.

We sat in silence for a while till Momma said, "I gotta get back to work, Beauty. And you gotta go back to school."

"Okay," I said.

Then Momma kissed me goodbye at the screen door of the Green River Soda Fountain and Drug Store and we went our separate ways.

✳

I didn't go back to school. I walked the long way home and hid myself up in my room. Thank goodness Grandma was at work, too. I heard her and Momma come in the house at different times, right about dinnertime, but I didn't call to them the way I usually do when they get home. No. I kept myself hidden and listened in on everything they said, lurking behind doors and around corners and stuff. They must be used to me spying, though. They spoke so soft I couldn't make out anything but the murmur of their voices.

While they were busy somewhere else, I ventured into the kitchen. I thought for sure I'd starve to death if I didn't. I wasn't planning to show up for supper. I packed myself some of Momma's restaurant quality food on a long cake pan and then hid it all in my closet, just in case someone came to my room for a visit. I didn't want them to *know* I was eating. But no one stopped by. Momma must have been madder than a disturbed water moccasin.

A little later, I heard Jamie downstairs. The sun was making a fast getaway, hurrying to rest on the other side of the

Gulf. This time I crouched in the hallway just outside the living room, listening in on Momma and Grandma and my teacher good and hard. I heard plenty, too. Patches, anyway.

"She did what?"

"*No* one was nice...?"

"And we believe in..."

More mumbling. Then, "*Beauty* did that?"

I'd heard enough. I made my way back up to my room and crawled into bed.

The saddest song I'd ever composed started in my head. I'm quite sure that no one has ever thought up a more mournful verse to "On Top of Old Smoky" than I did that night:

I am a big loser,
I see it right now.
Like some kids have told me
I'm dumb as a cow.

For being all bratty
To the girl at my school,
The truth is real clear now,
I broke our first rule.

chapter 6

You *will* go to school," Momma said, anger streaming out her eyes, "and you will *not* do what you did yesterday." Grandma stood tough behind Momma, strengthening her—though the last thing Momma needed was more power.

"Beauty, I did not raise you to be anything but the best flower on the tree."

"That's right," Grandma said.

I would have nodded, but my heart didn't even get a chance to beat again before Momma jumped back in. "*You,*" she said, her finger pointing straight at me, "are a McElwrath. And if nothing else, we have dignity."

"Amen," Grandma said.

"Now I expect that you will act like you are from this family and you will never, not ever in the rest of your life, do anything like what you did to that poor girl yesterday."

"I still cannot believe it," Grandma said.

If I hadn't known better, I'd have thought Grandma had been coaching Momma. And maybe she had. But Momma was stinking good at being the guilt queen all on her own.

"And you knowing what it's like to feel left out," Momma said.

"But—"

"Don't you argue with me," Momma said. "Now get your tail out to the bus stop and remember who you are."

"But—"

"Don't you 'but' me."

"Pretty is, Beauty," Grandma said. "Pretty is."

I headed out the door, my arms empty since I'd left all my schoolbooks in my classroom. I looked back once. Both Momma and Grandma stood on the porch, barring my way back to the safety of my bedroom. Anger glittered in their eyes.

Down the driveway I went. The river wasn't that far off, and I had to fight not to run toward it. But how could I, with Momma and Grandma both watching me like they could read my very thoughts?

The sun poured down warm on my shoulders. "Darn them both to heck," I said, kicking at the sandy driveway. Ahead, a slender green snake hurried from sight into the tall grass.

The lecture had started the moment I got up that morning and had kept up all the way through breakfast. Scared as I was to go to school, I could not wait to get out of the Devil's Den of

Lecturing. If only I could have made my way to a safe place. Like the special spot by the river where I talk to Great-Granny Dorothy Lu Lu. Or even back to bed.

What did either one of them know about me and what I was feeling? "That pretty-is motto is just crap," I said out loud, kicking the dirt. "Crap."

I made it to the bus stop just as the bus pulled up. I trudged up the stairs and dropped into a seat near the front.

Surprise of surprises, not one person spoke to me, not even the driver.

✳

I had to have a note to get back into school since I had just run off like that the day before. I dropped it off with Mr. Fish, the school secretary.

Momma's note was right to the point:

Dear Principal Haddon,

Beauty was overcome with a case of homesickness and guilt yesterday. She won't be leaving school grounds again without permission, and I mean it.

Sincerely, Nina McElwrath

In slow motion, I walked to class. If I had the nerve to turn around and walk back out, I could go straight home. Both Momma and Grandma would be at work by now.

But before I could escape again, I encountered one of the many problems that come up when your mother is dating your sixth-grade teacher.

Mr. Borget was standing in the hall just outside the classroom door. "Glad to have you back, Beauty," he said.

"Thanks," I said.

"Hope we have a better day today."

I didn't say it, but I thought, *Me, too.*

A few kids were at their desks, stowing their backpacks under their chairs and talking to each other and pretty much ignoring me. *If only our little town had more kids my age,* I thought. *Then I'd have more chance of making a friend. Please, God, let me have friends before I'm forty-three.* Then I folded my arms on my desktop and plunked my head down.

Even though I wasn't looking, I could tell when Alane came into the room because the other kids got quiet. "Hi, Mr. Borget," she said in this real happy voice.

"Alane," he said, all cheerful like everything was A-okay. "How are you this morning?"

"Just great," Alane said.

A moment later, I felt a tap on my shoulder.

"Is it all right if I sit next to you?" Alane's voice again.

Without even looking up, I said, "Sure." I was glad my face was down. I felt it turn at least four shades of red.

Alane settled into her chair. Then she whispered, "Mr. Borget told me you're the nicest person in this room. And he said you have the nicest family in town. Are you related to him or something?"

I took a deep breath and, with great effort, pulled my head up off my desk. It wasn't even 8:30 in the morning and already I was exhausted. "Or something," I said with a sorta smile.

Alane gave me a smile back. I noticed her braces had pink and purple ties. "Well, that sounds mysterious," she said.

"Teachers are never mysterious," I said. But I didn't mean to say that at all. I didn't even know why those words came out of my mouth.

She grinned again.

The class was filling up now. Most of the kids stared at Alane when they came in. Cody didn't even look at her. Maria and Dolly and Chalice took the long way around the room like they didn't want to get close to her.

Alane, though, chattered on. "In Oklahoma most of my teachers were boring," she said. "Or just plain freaked out about having me in their classrooms. I remember Ms. Dixon was afraid I would croak in her science lab."

"What do you mean, croak?" I said. Nervousness poured into me like cold water into a glass. I wanted to stare at Alane, and ask her questions about why she looked the way she did. But that would be rude. Besides, I didn't have the nerve to ask anyone much of anything.

"Oh, you know," Alane said. "Die. Have a heart attack or a stroke. Wouldn't it be scary to have a kid die on you like that? And right there in your classroom, too. That would be the worst thing, don't you think?"

I gave an almost nod, then frowned. "Why in the world would your teacher worry about that? You're way too…" Without meaning to, I hesitated. "You know, way too young."

"That's what I told *her*, but—"

A folded-up piece of paper hit Alane. It bounced off her shoulder and landed on the floor right between our desks. Stretching out her ancient-looking hand, she made a grab for the paper before I could stop her.

My mouth went dry. "Hey," I said. "Don't look at it."

But Alane had already straightened up, with effort, and unfolded the paper. She glanced at it and folded it again. Then, in a creaky, old lady sort of way, she got up out of her chair, shuffled to the trash can by the door, and threw the note away.

chapter 7

lane came back to her chair, rocking from side to side like maybe her hips were attached wrong. She was so small. Delicate, even. She eased herself down and said to me in a loud voice, "It's okay. I'm used to this."

Used to what? I almost said. But I knew. I hated to admit it to myself, but Alane was handling this outcast thing a lot better than I was.

Morning announcements came on over the intercom. Ryan walked into class late. Mr. Borget sat on his desk, swinging his legs like he was five or something. The smell of Thursday meatloaf made its way down to our classroom, though we were still hours away from lunchtime.

"All right," our teacher said, slapping his hands together. "Yesterday was our first day together. I want to take the beginning of class today to get to know each of you better. Get out some paper and write a page about yourselves. What you like, what you want to become, what scares you. I want each person in this classroom to know who you are when you sit down."

"We have to write them standing up?" Ben Bascom asked.

"No, Ben," Mr. Borget said. "You have to *read* them while you're standing up."

Read standing up? In front of people? My heart thumped.

"I love this kind of stuff," Alane said to me.

I looked at her, wide-eyed.

"Out loud?" Ben asked.

"Right." Mr. Borget gave the class a grin that showed all his teeth.

Jim Brady, the shortest boy in our grade, said, "We've been going to school together forever, Mr. Borget. We already know each other."

"No, you don't," Alane said, turning in her chair to face the back of the classroom. "You don't know *me*. I'm new here."

"Who wants to know you?" I heard someone whisper. I'm not sure who it was. Some girl. Why couldn't they keep their stupid mouths shut?

Alane gave me a smile. Those braces of hers were so strange on such an old-looking person. Something pinched at my heart.

Mr. Borget must not have heard the whisperer because he kept right on talking. "Alane's right," he said. "And *I* don't know the rest of you. While I've taught some of your brothers and sisters, that doesn't mean I know what *you* want to do with *your* lives. So, get out some paper and start writing. Writing what you know is easy. Don't worry about spelling. Write as fast as you can. You have fifteen minutes. Go."

I can't do this, I thought. My hands were already sweating.

Alane started writing like crazy.

My pencil was sharp from not using it yesterday. I tore a piece of paper from my new spiral notebook. "College ruled this year," Grandma had said when she handed me the stack, "because you are going to make something of yourself."

Just write, I told myself. *Then if Jamie calls on you, say no. He can't make you stand up in front of the class. You don't have to do anything...*

That's when I saw the magnifying glass, though for a second I had no idea what it was. You know, it just didn't make sense, a big Sherlock Holmes magnifying glass right in the middle of class. Alane had a tight hold on it, her left hand grasping the black handle. She held it in front of her face, real close to the page, a gel pen in her other hand.

She can't see, I realized. *Even with her glasses on.* That shook me up good. The other kids were going to have a field day with this.

My pencil trembled when I put the point down on the sheet of notebook paper. If there had been a thought about what to write in my head before, it was gone now. All I could think about was the time when Maria found out Momma was working at Dickie's. "Why's she doing a man's job?" she'd asked me.

"It's a job," I had said, as casual as when Momma had told us. She'd come home and announced, "I found work. It's at the gas station in town, but it's a job. Now maybe I can put some money aside and one day do what I love best: cook."

"But it's a *man's* job," Maria had said. "Doesn't she come home greasy and dirty?"

I shook my head. "Not really."

"Stinky?"

"Sometimes her hands smell like gas," I'd said.

And that was the end. The next day everyone in our grade knew all about my mom and her smelly hands.

A magnifying glass, I knew, would be worse than a mother with a job at the gas station. A magnifying glass that wasn't being used during science class meant sure death to a girl's social career. Worse than being shy, even. I turned around to see if anyone had noticed. They had. Kids were staring and whispering. Even Cody looked at Alane kind of funny.

"Beauty," Mr. Borget said from his desk, and nodded at my paper.

I took a deep breath and started writing. Before, I had wanted to say something about how Momma wanted to open a restaurant and how generations have lived in my home, always women, and how my grandmother was younger than some of the mothers of the kids in this room. I could have written about

how my father left before I was born because he was just fifteen himself and how I didn't miss him because I had Momma
and Grandma to make up for a dad who in my mind would
always be fifteen—just three years older than me. But I didn't.

"My name is Beauty McElwrath," I wrote. A gypped feeling
sat in my chest, but I wrote anyway. And I wrote the thing I
write best: a song.

> *I don't get this new girl.*
> *It doesn't seem fair.*
> *The only thing nice there*
> *Is her pretty brown hair.*
>
> *How will she survi-ive*
> *Here at this school?*
> *They already thi-ink*
> *That she isn't cool.*

Then, because I could never read that in class, I scribbled
down the bare essentials about myself, the simple facts that
everyone in this class already knew.

Except Alane.

chapter 8

Time," Mr. Borget said. "I'll start." He took out his
paper, and blew it off, like maybe it'd collected a load
of dust in the fifteen minutes it sat on his desk. Then
he read about how he'd lived in the East all his life, but not
always here in Florida. And how teaching was one of the
coolest things he'd ever done. And how he used to visit Europe
every summer but how that had changed just two months ago,
because he'd stayed here in Green River. Right then Jamie (at
that moment it was definitely Jamie, not Mr. Borget) peeked a
look at me. He had a small smile on his lips.

I felt my skin start to burn, like when I've been at the beach
too long and I know before even going home that I have cooked
myself. Why did I always have to get so embarrassed?

"It's your turn now, class," he said when he had finished.
"I'm just going to pick a name at random. Be prepared to come

up here and read what you have written. Speak up so we can all hear."

My breath came in nervous little gasps. Why was he making us do this?

"Sarah Brunstrom."

Sarah stood and cleared her throat. "Well, okay," she said, and read her essay about wanting to raise quarter horses.

Don't call on me, I thought the whole time Sarah was reading. *Please not me.* Then something worse came into my head. Alane. *Please don't call on me or Alane. Please not her, either.*

Maria was next. She practically pranced to the front of the room. Then she looked at everyone with a smug little smile. I figured she might as well go ahead and take a bow before she even started. How could she feel so confident up there? I expected her to write about how she just knew all those dance lessons would come in handy and how she'd move away to New York and become a famous dancer. But no, she just told us how all she wanted in life was to get married and have kids. She looked right at Ryan when she said, "My husband and I will have three children, two boys and a girl."

For some reason this struck me as funny. I fanned my face with my hand and tried not to giggle. She kept staring at Ryan. When I caught a glimpse of him, his face was all red. A nervous bubble of laughter rose up behind my tongue. I heard Alane giggle, too.

Vickie Finlay got called on next. She wanted to be an architect. Then it was Cody's turn, who talked about being an ultimate skateboarding guy, and not a word about me and all the fun we used to have together.

Three more people went. Then Mr. Borget called on me.

"Come on up, Miss McElwrath," he said.

I shook my head no.

Chalice snorted.

"I can't," I said. "I can't go up there."

"Then stay in your seat," Alane said. "Is that okay, Mr. Borget?"

He grinned. "Yes, I suppose it is, Alane."

I looked at my paper. The song was scratched out. "It's short," I said. Then I took a deep breath and dived in. "My name is Beauty McElwrath and I have always lived in our two-story house near the Green River. I have no full brothers or sisters and my father lives in Ohio. But I am happy here. I love sitting in my favorite spot on the river and driving along the beach at night. And I love my family." I left out Momma's restaurant and how much I wanted her to get it someday, and I left out our Great-Granny Dorothy Lu Lu, too. "That's it," I said.

Alane clapped her hands. "Good job, Beauty."

"I didn't know it could be that short," Josh Terry said. "Man, I wasted fifteen minutes."

Mr. Borget ignored him, but I saw him smiling. Then he called on Alane.

She got to her feet and made her way to Jamie's side. She was about a foot and half taller than his desk. She faced the class, cleared her throat, and started to read, holding that big round magnifying glass close to her face again.

"If I had all the time in the world," she read, her voice smooth like water, "I would write a book, because I love words." She smiled at the class. Her braces caught a bit of light. "I think they're beautiful." Then she started reading again. My heart banged like it was *me* reading out loud to everyone. "Books have been my friends when people wouldn't. Books are always kind. They can make a person feel better. They can keep you from being lonely."

On she went about how books can take you so many magical places and show you things you might never have imagined. She said that her biggest dream was to write a book that other people would read someday. I listened to her soft voice and I knew right then that Alane meant what she said. Maria *might* marry Ryan Harding, and Sarah *might* raise quarter horses, and Cody *might* be a famous skateboarder, but Alane Shriver *would* write a book.

The thing that I noticed as Alane read in front of the whole class, that big magnifying glass up to her eyes, was that she never once mentioned her disease. She didn't complain about her looks, or the funny way she walked, or her almost-blind eyes. She didn't say a word about how hard it was to write with her crooked fingers or about how short she was or about her pinched nose. She just talked about being a writer.

"That's it, I guess," she said.

Mr. Borget beamed at her. "Terrific, Alane," he said. "I bet you do get that novel written."

"I'm going to try," she said, then hobbled to her seat.

Just before she sat down she turned to face the class again. "Oh, and I have an announcement to make."

Everyone in the room was dead silent.

"Go ahead," Mr. Borget said.

She gazed at the class a moment. "I wear a wig," she said, then sat down.

"A wig?" Maria said. "A *wig?*"

A low murmur spread through the room as the kids marveled at this revelation.

Mr. Borget looked like I felt. Bug-eyed. "Well," he said.

Alane stood up again. "I wear it because I can't grow hair. And at my last school it bothered people when they found out this isn't mine." Her gnarled hand, the one not holding the magnifying glass, lifted a few strands of the wig hair. "So now you all know."

Yes sir, buddy, now we knew.

Alane plopped down in her chair. Then she leaned toward

me and said, "I *am* going to write something, even if there's no time for a whole book."

Someone in the back—maybe Maria—said, "She's making friends with Beauty. The losers are together."

I pulled away from Alane and looked up at Mr. Borget, who had heard some of the whisperings. He seemed furious, like he was getting ready to explode.

"Good," I thought. *"Tear 'em apart."*

But he didn't. He just took a deep breath and turned his back on the class.

chapter 9

My great-grandmother, Dorothy Lu Lu McElwrath, the woman whose shyness skipped two generations and landed on me, drowned in the river behind our house when Momma was just seventeen years old. By that time I'd been alive for almost three years. Ever since I could go out on my own, I've made it a habit to frequent Great-Granny Dorothy Lu Lu's drowning spot. Or at least the place where she was found, caught amongst all the debris and roots of a tree, once the high water went down. I feel a certain kinship to my great-grandmother. We are linked by both her life and her death.

Grandma always says her momma was the best woman around. And I believe that. How else would Grandma and Momma be the way *they* are if Great-Granny Dorothy Lu Lu hadn't been a terrific person herself?

Anyway, it was to that spot on the river I headed as soon

as I got home from school that afternoon. I didn't even stop to get cookies or anything. Just threw my backpack on the front porch and hightailed it out to the river.

"Great-Granny Dorothy Lu Lu," I said as I hurried to our meeting place. "We have got to talk."

Sure, Momma could talk good and long. But I needed someone to *listen*. And believe you me, Momma always has an answer whether there's a question or not. Besides, Great-Granny Dorothy Lu Lu never argues with me.

The smell of oak trees and warmed earth and distant water was heavy in the air. The closer I got to the river, the thicker the trees became. Soon there was no grass under my feet, just dark earth covered with fallen leaves. I saw a racing snake, long and thin and striped, heading toward the river, too. But when I got close, he took off in the opposite direction.

I hoped the long walk would clear my mind. I didn't want to see Alane in my head anymore. I didn't want to see that magnifying glass or think about that long hair or remember how everyone had treated her after the wig announcement.

When I arrived at my spot, I settled on the bank in a big square of hot sunlight and let my legs dangle over the edge. Just a bit down the river, not even twenty-five feet away, was the place where Great-Granny Dorothy Lu Lu got caught. From where I sat, I could see it all: the way the river had cut deep into the ground making a wide U, the exposed tree roots reaching for a hold in the earth, the sand along the banks, the gold of the sun on the green water. This time of year it was shallow. But in the spring and during hurricane season and on the rainy days of winter the river rose high. Sometimes it got high enough to sweep up and over its bank, though that didn't happen often.

"Great-Granny Dorothy Lu Lu," I said into the warm air of the afternoon. "You here?"

No answer. There never is, but that's okay. I've been talking to her for so long I'm sure she's listening.

"I just don't get it." My voice sounded hushed, as if the leaves had made a blanket to cover my words. I could hear the *slip, slip, slip* of the water, the call of the mockingbirds, and every once in a while the buzz of a fat, green horsefly.

"I have too much worry in me, Great-Granny Lu Lu. I don't even know that I can talk about it all." I started out slow, hoping to get an answer or two. "There's this new girl at school. And people are not nice to her."

My words floated in the air like a light cloud. I imagined Great-Granny Dorothy Lu Lu out here with me. I saw her the way she was in that old picture that hangs in the living room. All smiles, looking at my mother—still just a girl herself—holding me on her hip.

In my imagination, my great-grandmother smiled at me, eager to hear all about Alane. According to family photos, and Momma's and Grandma's memories, my great-grandmother was a real smiler.

I closed my eyes tight. From across the river I heard the frogs calling out their deep-throated songs for rain. "Great-Granny Dorothy Lu Lu, Alane looks so old. She looks older than any of our relatives, no matter how far back in pictures a person can go." I pictured Alane standing in front of the class, her paperlike skin, her dark, long-haired wig, her fingers bent all funny.

A slight breeze rustled through the trees, like a hand stroking the leaves.

"Why, Great-Granny Dorothy Lu Lu? Why is she like that?"

And then, like I sometimes do, I started missing this great-grandmother I'd known for less than three years. Or at least the telling I knew of her—and what I'd made up on my own.

"Jamie wants me to be friends with Alane," I told her, tears burning my eyes. "He's not said as much, but I know. I can tell by looking at him."

I cried then. I mean, I sat there on the river—right where Great-Granny Dorothy Lu Lu McElwrath had drowned—and cried my head off. With my tears came the words of the kids in class. You know, the mean things they whispered about Alane. Then I thought about how Alane wanted to be a writer, and I bawled even harder because I knew if she *really* wanted to write a book it would be extra hard because how could she see to write it?

"Why can't any doctors help her?" I said. "It's not fair."

Two things happened at that very moment, and I'm not so

sure my dead great-grandmother didn't have anything to do with them.

The first thing was the light that went on in my head. It showed me that what was going on with Alane was a lot worse than what was going on with me and *my* puny life. I might be shy, but I could see just fine. I might have no friends, but I didn't look like a dried-up old lady. I might be scared to death to talk to people, but I didn't have to wear a wig. Grandma's "pretty is" motto and all her harping started making a lot of sense.

The second thing was the voice. "Beauty," it said, all faraway and soft and watery like. A voice that could have belonged to a drowned woman. A voice that—

"Hey, Beauty, I thought you quit coming out here."

I screamed like I was being attacked by a nest of hornets and jerked my head around.

There in the scattered light of the setting sun stood Cody, his mouth hanging open with surprise, his blond hair tucked behind his ears. And next to him was Ryan Harding.

chapter 10

I can tell you right now, from my own personal experience, that some things make people stop crying faster than others.

I had been ready to lie back on the warm soil on that early evening by the river and continue to feel sorry for myself, but having two boys from school—and one of them Cody—show up at this very private moment stopped the tears quick. It also gave me a flash of courage.

"What are you doing on my property, Jared Cody Nelson?" I leapt to my feet and stuck my fists to my hips like Momma does when she's riled up

"We heard something...," Cody said.

"It sounded like a baby...," Ryan said.

" ...crying," Cody said.

"You can see," I said, straightening up tall, "that there is no baby here." I wiped at my wet cheeks. I could feel the flush start up my neck, as usual.

"But *you've* been crying," Ryan said. "You okay?"

I dusted off the seat of my pants. A few dead leaves scattered to the ground. "I am fine."

"Let's get out of here," Cody said to Ryan in a low voice. He grabbed at Ryan's blue shirt and pulled him back a few steps.

"I thought you were going to show me your make-out place," Ryan said. "I thought you were gonna show me where they found the dead lady."

Without meaning to, I gasped. *Cody couldn't have. He wouldn't have...*

"You didn't," I said. Even though I could tell my eyes were swollen and my nose was probably crimson-colored, and even though I hadn't talked to Cody in a long while and I'd never really talked to Ryan, I marched right up to Cody and shoved him a good one in the chest.

"Whoa," Ryan said. A grin spread out on his face. "She's the one, isn't she? You were making out here with Beauty."

"Wait a minute," Cody said. He held his hands up to both me and Ryan.

"That is not even a little bit true and you know it." I shoved Cody again, hard.

"Can I bring Maria out here, you think?" Ryan said. He bent forward, like he was asking *me* permission.

"No," I said. "This is my place."

"Let's go," Cody said to Ryan. Now his face was red. Well, good. He should be embarrassed. Why should I be the only one?

"You better go," I said. "Right now."

"What about the dead lady?" Ryan asked.

"That"—my voice was loud—"was my great-grandmother. She drowned."

"Oh." Ryan looked at me wide-eyed. Night was coming in over us, dark and heavy like a quilt. Mosquitoes buzzed. "I didn't know the dead person was related to you."

"Well, *he* did." With my chin I motioned to Cody. "And we did *not* make out," I said. "He's got a huge imagination."

"Sorry," Cody said. He looked down at his feet.

"Yeah, I bet," I said.

Cody pushed Ryan ahead of him and they walked away along the riverbank. I followed just a bit behind them, staying hidden in the trees.

I heard Ryan's voice through the thick leaves. "So did ya kiss her, or didn't ya?"

"Shut up," Cody said. "I—"

"He didn't tell you," I yelled after them, "because it was a big fat lie!"

"You know, she is kinda cute. I never noticed before."

"Cute? I don't know about that. But she's mean as a snake."

"And loud."

"I'll say."

"I never noticed that before, either. She's pretty quiet at school."

I'd heard enough. How humiliating, right in front of Great-Granny Dorothy Lu Lu. Cody had ruined my talk with my dead best friend.

I felt tired. I didn't have the energy to slap at mosquitoes when they landed on me, but I forced my heavy legs to carry me back toward our house.

Home was where I needed to be. With Momma and Grandma. And dinner on the table, hot and waiting.

✳

"Oh, stinking great," I said when our front yard came into view. There, parked in the dirt drive, was my teacher's rickety old car—the object that had first brought Momma and him together that afternoon last May at Dickie's Gas and Other Services.

"So much for private time with family," I said as I passed the battered Toyota.

I tiptoed onto the porch, grabbed my backpack that still waited for me on the top step, and opened the door without a sound. From the front hall I could hear Momma, Jamie, and Grandma laughing. Momma was in the middle of one of her stories.

"He marched right into the gas station, big as life," Momma said.

"Are you sure?" Grandma said, her voice wheezy from laughing.

"It must have been a trick of light," Jamie said.

"I swear," Momma said, "it *was* Elvis. And he had one of those paintings of himself on black velvet sitting in the backseat with the shoulder belt strapped across it."

They all laughed again.

I crept toward the dining room. If I could just get a small peek of dinner...

With care I pushed the swinging door open and found myself peering right into Grandma's face.

"Beauty," she said. "I thought I heard you out there. Where have you been? We waited dinner like one pig waits for another." Grandma grinned. "Get on in here before everything's gone. You know dinner's at 6:30 sharp."

"I lost track of time," I said. I pulled my chair out from the table. There was no way I could talk about my awful day now, not with my teacher right next to Momma.

"Glad you decided to come home," Momma said. "Jamie wanted to talk to you about something."

I stopped an inch from plopping my behind on the chair. Why couldn't he just talk to me at school, like a normal teacher? All I'd hoped for was a little peace and quiet and some of Momma's secret ingredient fried chicken, and now I was going to have to listen to a lecture.

"Good to see you, Beauty," Jamie said.

My back end hovered above the chair. "Uh huh."

"Sit down, girl," Grandma said. "Eat up."

I sat. Grandma filled a plate for me—a pile of corn pie, Momma's complicated fruit salad with nuts, and a golden chicken leg.

"There's something I need to talk to you about," he said.

I knew that already. I looked at my mother's boyfriend and started to pick up the chicken leg.

"It's about Alane Shriver."

I put the chicken down. *Duh.*

"I met her parents at the gas station," Momma said. "Nice folks. From Oklahoma, right?"

"Right," Jamie said.

One thing about Momma—and another good reason she should open a restaurant—is that she knows everybody in town. We only have that one gas station, so people always fill up there. And she talks to everyone the whole time she pumps their gas or washes their windshields.

"Here's the deal, Beauty." Jamie leaned his elbows on the table.

I stared just an inch to the left of his eyes.

"I need to ask you a big favor," he said. "Maybe it's not fair. Maybe I shouldn't do this. But you heard those kids in class today."

I nodded.

"Children can be so cruel," Grandma said.

Momma dropped her fork onto her plate with a clatter. "Mommy," she said. "I hate it when people say that. Children can also be terrific."

"You're right," Grandma said. "But they sometimes do dumb things." She and Momma glared at me good and hard.

"What?" I said.

Jamie talked over my family. "She's lonely, Beauty."

I pushed the corn pie around on my plate.

"And I think you know how that feels."

I guess that was obvious. I gave Jamie another weak nod.

"So maybe the two of you could be friends."

Outside, heat lightning crackled. Frogs sang loud for rain that might not come. The dinner smells swirled in the heavy air spun by the ceiling fan.

"Look, Beauty. She's new here. She didn't have friends in Oklahoma because of her...her condition. You have no idea how hard it is for her. Imagine how it would be to look like that." Now Jamie was talking a mile a minute.

I slumped in my chair, real low so that only the top of my head from my eyes up showed.

"Listen to Jamie," Momma said, even though I hadn't done anything *but* listen since I came into the room.

He gestured toward me. "You're such a pretty girl. And you always will be."

I squeezed my eyes shut.

"You'll live a full, happy life. Maybe you'll have an important job someday. And maybe you'll get married and have babies."

Not to Cody Nelson, I thought. *I won't be marrying him, that's for sure.*

"I hope so," Grandma said, almost whispering. "It'd be nice if someone in our family got married."

"And stayed married," Momma said. They gave each other the Old Eyeball.

"That's not going to happen with Alane, Beauty. Not any of it." Jamie's voice sounded misty. "But if you wanted, you could make her life here good for however long she stays around."

I wanted to tell them that I didn't even have the courage to try making friends with a person who looked normal, much less with someone who didn't. Instead, I rolled my eyes. Momma saw me, too, though I'm not quite sure how, since she was exchanging looks with Grandma at that exact moment.

"Beauty McElwrath," Momma said, her voice all surprised sounding. "If I could wash your eyes out with soap right this second, you know I would."

She didn't have a clue how hard this was for me. She didn't know I was a little afraid of Alane. And sorry for her, like Jamie. And confused.

"But Momma—"

"Don't you 'but Momma' me," she said. "You know how much I hate it when you roll your eyes." She gave Jamie a small smile like she was apologizing for me. Then she took a deep breath.

"Now, Momma," I said. "Please. I already know what you're going to say."

"Then listen to your teacher," Momma said, "and listen to me. Help that poor little girl if you can."

I rolled my eyes again, but this time I did it staring at the uneaten food on my plate. If I was going to do anything, anything at all, I'd do it because *I* wanted to.

chapter
11

I ran up to my bedroom, without eating a thing, mind you, even though I was starving for some of Mama's fried chicken.

I opened my window and looked out at the big oak.

Our tin roof, in the middle of a summer day, can get hot enough to fry an egg. I know this for a fact. Use a little butter, and it won't stick, either. Anyway, out the window I went and onto the roof, still radiating a little of the September warmth. My bare feet kept me from slipping.

The moon looked like a huge paper circle cut from cloudy paper. I could see the branches of the oak tree almost as clear as day.

I reached for the limb that sweeps toward my bedroom window and jumped the two feet over to it.

I've been doing this for so long, my feet know what to do. Of course, Momma doesn't know that I sneak out sometimes.

In fact, she doesn't know a lot of things about me. Like how I sometimes go down to the river when it runs high and floods the banks or how I take her car out late at night after the house has gone quiet or how sometimes I block the number on our phone and call Fat Sam's and order pizzas that I never intend to buy. That's just the beginning of my many entertainments. When you're a loner, you have to invent pastimes. I've made up a saying: "What your momma don't know can't get you in trouble." I may be shy, but when I'm all by myself I can do just about anything.

The rough bark of the oak tree felt nice and familiar under my hands and bare feet. It didn't take me long to scramble down. Around the house I went, quiet as a cat, past the two plastic pink flamingos that stare off into the woods. Past the azalea bushes planted close to the house, hiding the way it stands stacked on cinder blocks. Past another huge oak where Momma built me a tree house high in the limbs.

By the time I got beyond that tree I could hear Momma and Jamie talking in low voices. About me and Alane, I was sure. I decided, coming around the house, to set a few things straight with them. First, I needed to tell them how my heart jerked around in my chest when I even thought of talking to any of the kids at school. Then, I needed to tell them that they should back off and let me make a decision or two for myself.

Ahead of me, the light from the front porch jabbed into the dark and lit up a rectangle of earth.

I tiptoed, edging to the corner of the house, moving as slow as a slug.

"I know we haven't known each other that long," Jamie said.

True, though I wasn't sure what this had to do with Alane and me.

Momma let out a little giggle. And I mean that. A little-girl *giggle*. For a minute I felt confused. We McElwraths *never* giggle. As far as I'm concerned, it's against our religion.

And what did giggling have to do with me and the new girl? I tried to see around the corner with just my right eyeball. Couldn't do it.

"I've tried that once," Momma said. "It lasted three weeks."

Tried what?

"But this will last forever, I know it. I believe in forever, Nina."

Huh? Leading with my left big toe, I began to make my way into the box of light so I could see a bit more of what was going on. And there I saw my mother—at the ancient age of twenty-six—in a lip lock with my teacher. They were *kissing!*

My brain stumbled. How did kissing have anything to do with my problem?

Why? Why would they—I mean, I knew they were friends, but I'd never seen my mother, you know, kiss someone who wasn't related to us. Especially not *my teacher*. And certainly not on the lips and on our front porch. Jamie and Momma were just friends. Not kissers.

Wait a minute…wait a minute…wait a *minute*.

It took great strength for me not to scream my face off. Strength that lasted about five seconds.

I hollered so loud I felt my own lips vibrate.

Momma's and Jamie's faces moved apart in fear. Neither one of them could have looked more surprised if I had jumped out with a torch and started them both on fire.

"Beauty McElwrath!" Momma yelled so loud that Jamie could probably see that dangly thing in the back of her throat. "I cannot believe you are spying on us!"

"I cannot believe you are making out!" I hollered back. "Aren't you too old for that?"

"I'm twenty-six!" Momma yelled. "That's not too old to kiss a man!"

"I don't care if you're a million. You happen to be with my sixth-grade teacher. And you two are just friends. *Friends.*"

By now Momma had stomped her way to the edge of the porch. "Get to your room right now!" she yelled at me through the screen.

"I'm going! And I'm stopping in the kitchen for cleanser so I can scrub out my brain."

And I did. Well, I didn't scrub out my brain, but I marched around to the back and into the kitchen, slamming the door as

I went. From the living room Grandma called out, "Like my momma said, 'Put your head where it ain't wanted and you're likely to catch a bullet.'" Then she laughed.

She always laughs at my misfortune. If I had a regular grandmother she'd have been out on the porch with a broom, beating the two of them apart. But no. My grandmother *encourages* her own daughter to misbehave. And on top of that, she's always spouting those old sayings that no one in the world has ever heard of but herself and Great-Granny Dorothy Lu Lu. Will *I* be like that when I'm forty-five?

I stormed out of the kitchen, up the stairs, and into my room. On the way I managed to slam two more doors.

"The nerve!" I shouted out the window. "How rude can you get?" But because my room sits at the back of the house, I wasn't sure either one of them had heard my exact words. So I hollered louder. "That guy is my *teacher!* You don't *kiss* teachers. It's *wrong!* Wrong, I tell you. Teachers do *not* kiss. Not friends. Not anyone. Ever. And above all, not *my mother!* Mothers do not kiss teachers. They should not kiss—"

I had just taken a breath to hurl some more outraged words out the window when my bedroom door popped open and hit the wall.

"Quit that hollering," Grandma said. "You want the neighbors to hear?"

"We live half a mile from the nearest neighbors," I said. "And yes, I hope they can hear me."

"It just so happens," Grandma said, "I don't give a hoot about the neighbors. All this howling is driving me mad."

I squinched my eyes into tiny slits to keep back the all-of-a-sudden tears. "You didn't see what I just saw. You didn't see *them*. It's bad enough for me at school already. When this gets out..."

"Beauty, your mother deserves something good in her life."

I threw my hands up in the air. "You sound like a bad movie, Grandma. *Your mother deserves something good in her life.* She *has* good things. Plenty of good things. She's got me." I poked a finger at my chest. "And you, too." I poked it toward Grandma. "What more does she need?" Now *I* sounded like a bad movie.

"Jamie is a good man."

I turned my back on Grandma.

"And he has never been anything but good to you."

That was true, I had to admit. Except when he didn't mind his own business. Like about me and Alane.

"They were using tongues out there." I folded my arms and turned to meet Grandma head on. I couldn't look her in the eye, though. I was just so, well, embarrassed by the whole thing.

Grandma got into my face, avoiding all personal space rules that should be observed, especially during family arguments. "This is not like you at all, Beauty."

But I couldn't stop. "No!" I stamped my foot. "If anyone at school finds out about this, I am dead in the water."

Grandma heaved a big sigh and hugged me close to her. "Ah, Beauty," she said, patting my back.

I bawled for a long time. And I let Grandma pat down my frustration and sadness and worry. After a while, she started to leave the room but paused at the door, her hand on the knob, her long blond hair hanging smooth down her back.

"Beauty," she said. "Remember who you are. You know what our family believes. Your Great-Granny Dorothy Lu Lu taught you to be kind before you could even walk."

There it was again, haunting me. And me so tired I could hardly think.

Pretty is as pretty diz.

chapter 12

The memory has become real by all the telling and retelling. So real I can almost touch it. The memory is my story. The story of my birth and my naming.

This is the truth, the whole truth, and, well, I believe I have made myself clear.

From the moment I was born, Grandma (and everyone else present) always says there never was a prettier baby. There they were, Momma—of course—and Grandma and Great-Granny Dorothy Lu Lu, in the hospital over in Jacksonville. And every other female relative in my family, too. They'd crammed themselves into the pink and blue birthing room at the hospital that was decorated like someone might do a bedroom.

I, of course, was busy being born, traveling into the world—and taking my time, to hear Momma tell it. But I've heard the details so many times I bet I could draw a picture of what that room looked like, including the painting of the woman carrying the basket, with two geese beside her.

If I see anyone in my extended family who's older than twelve at a family reunion up in Tifton or down in Orlando or right here in my very own backyard, it does not fail that at least one individual will say, "Remember the evening Beauty was born?"

Anyway, all my relatives were crowded around Momma, who refused to get any painkillers, even to take the edge off. Great-Aunt Kyra and her family huddled in one corner of the room singing gospel music. Great-Aunt Sarah and her family stood by the window. They were all praying. Great-Aunt Cait sat in a rocker and knitted like crazy. Booties, for me. Her family sat on the floor around her. The room was jam-packed.

The doctor hollered for everybody to leave when the time came for me to be born, but not one person would budge. The two nurses tried to escort everyone from the room, but Momma wouldn't hear of it. "Dr. Ochoa," she said real loud, "I want my family nearby. I love them all dearly." And for some reason he let them stay. All of them in scrubs and face masks. All pressed against the walls—praying, knitting, and singing—waiting for me to come into the world.

Fifteen minutes later, on March 23 at 10:20 in the evening, I was born for just about everyone in the family to see. Great-aunts and children, quiet and staring. They all heard Dr. Ochoa say, "I have never seen such a beautiful newborn in all my days of delivering babies."

"Land a-mighty," the nurse said, "you're right."

Everyone in the room smiled, except me. I just yawned a big one, blinked a couple of times, and peed on the doctor.

"Give her a strong name," Great-Granny Dorothy Lu Lu said when she held me bundled in a warm pink blanket. "It'll give her character." She gave me my very first kiss.

"Give her a name that reminds her who she is," Grandma said. She was waiting her turn to hold me. It was Grandma who gave me my second kiss.

"Give her a name that reminds her of family," Great-Aunt Sarah said. She was bawling from happiness.

Momma, worn out from the delivery, said, "I'm calling her Beauty McElwrath. A name that does all three things."

And since my daddy was nowhere to be seen, and because he and his family were already on their way out of Green River, Momma got to make the final decision. I have regretted that since day one, I do believe. Who can live up to a name like that?

Sometimes I wonder if my name would have been different if my daddy had stayed around. Momma says no. She says Johnny Bennion wasn't much up to being a daddy, he being just fifteen himself. She lets me talk to him anytime I want. He works at a car dealership in Ohio and has three little boys. He always sounds a little embarrassed when I call.

But it's okay. Because Momma and me and Grandma, we got an okay thing here. Even with Jamie Borget pushing in a little too hard on the edges.

∗

At 4:44 in the a.m., I awoke with a start. It was like someone had tapped me on the shoulder. "Great-Granny Dorothy Lu Lu?" I let my voice out soft, not quite a whisper.

I lay in bed and let the wheels in my head turn. I thought about Cody telling Ryan that our talking place by the river was where he and I made out. I thought about Momma and Jamie kissing and us hollering at each other. I thought about Grandma saying Momma needed something good in her life. Wasn't I good enough for her? She said to me all the time, "Best friends, Beauty. You and I are best friends." Didn't she mean that anymore? Had Jamie taken my place?

I lay flat on my back, the covers half kicked off and dangling from my feet. I stared up at the dark ceiling and smelled the night fragrances of the river. Outside, not too far away, an owl hooted. A neighbor's dog barked. A sweet breeze pushed in through the window.

It was right then on that Saturday morning that I made up my mind to visit Alane. And not because of what anyone else told me I should do. I decided on my own. I needed a friend.

And so did she. And it might take me sifting around a little for courage. But I thought I was up to it.

Momma had Jamie now. Grandma had her sisters that she talked to on the phone. I had no one. And I knew Alane didn't either.

I got up, kicking the leftover covers to the floor, and went to the phone on my desk. I dialed information, jotted down the new listing for Shriver, then went to the window.

"Great-Granny Dorothy Lu Lu?" I whispered. "Are you out there somewhere?"

The moonlight washed the oak leaves over like they'd been dunked in milk. At long last I crawled into bed and tried to go back to sleep. The last four digits of Alane's phone number ran through my head. *Nineteen seventy-five. Nineteen seventy-five. Nineteen...*

chapter 13

hen it was morning, Alane's number still repeating in my brain. I walked to the phone and called her house. A woman answered on the third ring. "Hello?"

"Hi. May I please speak to Alane?" I stretched the long cord out so far that someone could have jumped rope. My hands felt slick with sudden sweat.

The woman hesitated a second, then said, "Why, yes. Of course." She covered the mouthpiece, but still I heard her call, "Laney!" Then she was back on the phone with me again. "May I tell her who's calling?"

I gripped the phone tighter so my hand would stop trembling. "My name is Beauty McElwrath. I'm in Alane's class at school."

"Oh," she said. "How nice of you to call."

In the front room I could hear Grandma talking about the benefits of Mary Kay moisturizer to Great-Aunt Sarah. Something about fine lines disappearing and about how she used the product and just look at her, she had a grandchild almost in her teens. Momma was home from the gas station. Good smells came from the kitchen.

"Hello?" Alane's voice was soft.

"Alane?" My voice sounded thin and shaky.

"Yes?"

"It's Beauty McElwrath from your class at school. You probably...um...don't remember me?" I stumbled over the words. Why, why, why couldn't I talk on the phone without an attack of the jitters?

"Of course I remember you," Alane said. "I sit right next to you in class."

"Yeah, that's me. I was wondering..." I took a deep breath and lowered my voice so that no one in the house could hear. "Um, I was wondering if you'd be interested in going on a beach drive a little later this evening."

Alane didn't answer, so I kept talking, fast but quiet. "Every once in a while, after my momma goes to bed, I borrow her car and ride out to the beach. It's just a half hour away from here. I'm a real good driver. I taught myself a year or two back when Momma was taking a correspondence course on mechanics. I learned to steer on my own. I've never been in even one wreck."

"You *drive?*" Alane's voice rose way up high, like she couldn't believe what I'd just said.

Well, truth be told, no one else in the world knows I'm a

midnight driver. Not even Cody. "Sure do," I said, beginning to wonder if I had made a mistake telling this to Alane. I held my breath waiting for her answer.

"That is so cool."

"So you'll go?" I asked.

"I'd love to. It sounds great."

"But...you know...we can't tell anyone."

"Right," Alane whispered. "When will you be by?"

"Close to midnight. Wear black, just in case. And sneakers, too. Sometimes there's broken glass on the beach. And bring a big towel."

"Check," Alane said.

*

If Momma ever knew I took the car at night, she'd bust a spleen. And a few blood vessels in her neck as well. And not just because I'm only twelve.

She bought her car a few years back when she got her job at Dickie's and started restoring it that very minute. She added stuff like fancy mirrors and new blue carpet, and she took out the old inlaid wood that had split and replaced it with stuff off another Cadillac on Dickie's back lot. She spent hours and hours working that car over. Waxing it, buffing it, fixing it, shining it, making it look like new. When it was finished, she christened it "Ringo." She won't let anyone drive ol' Ringo. Not even Grandma. Momma says Grandma wanted an orange Toyota truck and that's what she got, so she just better get used to the fact that Ringo is off-limits.

Grandma got the message.

But I didn't.

Like I said, I've been driving awhile now. And like sitting on my roof or wandering down to the river to talk to Great-Granny Dorothy Lu Lu, driving makes me relax. It's safe at night. Hardly anyone on the road. And people don't notice you as much.

Momma and Grandma turned in at 10:30 that night. When I heard Momma snoring, I got out of bed and dressed myself in an old black T-shirt and a pair of Momma's ancient sweat pants that are three inches too short for me. I pulled my hair into a ponytail, put on a baseball cap, and got out my favorite huge flashlight that's nearly as strong as a lighthouse's beam.

Then I waited.

chapter 14

At 11:45 p.m. sharp I crept down the stairs and into the kitchen where Momma's car keys hang from a big wooden key with cup hooks screwed into it. I let myself out the back door, because it squeaks less, and tiptoed to the garage.

Even if the moon hadn't been so bright, I could've found my way to our old garage just fine. I've been back here too many times to count. From the outside, the garage looks like our house, with an attic and all. On rainy summer days when I'm alone at home, I love to look through all the junk crammed into that attic. I keep waiting for the ghost of one of our long-gone relatives to visit me, to lead me to a secret stash of gold that was hidden before even Great-Granny Dorothy Lu Lu was born. It has yet to happen, but I haven't quit hoping. A kid could do a lot with some gold.

It didn't take me long to get to the garage and start the

car. Using the flashlight to point the way, I backed slow and easy down our long driveway. I made my shoulders relax and breathed in the rich smell of Momma's white leather car seats.

Once out to the bus stop, I turned on the car lights, then cruised into town, where the one traffic light at the center of Main and State glowed like a big red eye on a rope. I obeyed the thirty-five-mile-an-hour speed limit all the way to Alane's house, where I found her sitting on her front porch, wrapped in a blanket.

I pulled the car to a halt on her street right in front of her house, nerves thrumming. I'd turned off the headlights half a block back, just to be safe. But that didn't stop me from worrying that I might be pushing my luck a little too far this time. Alane lived in the new section of town, where the roads were smooth blacktop and tall streetlights cast glowing circles of orange onto the sidewalks. We were only four and a half blocks away from Maria's house.

"Alane." My loud whisper found its way to where she sat. She moved to her feet in slow motion, letting her blanket slip from her shoulders. Alane's pale face seemed to float above the lawn. The rest of her small body blended in with the night.

"I'm coming," she said, dragging the blanket with her. She moved like she didn't quite trust the ground, like it might swell up unexpectedly and cause her to fall.

Momma's old Cadillac made almost no noise. I waited in the

dark, my hands grasping the steering wheel, the car seat moved back a little because my legs are so much longer than Momma's. I watched as Alane picked her way to the car.

"I made it," she said, breathless.

At first I thought she meant the walk to the car. Then she held up the blanket, and I could see the pale blue yarn with silver threads running through it. "I crocheted this whole thing before my hands got too sore from arthritis. My mom helped a little bit." She grinned wide and the streetlight caught her braces.

"Get you and your blanket in here," I said, grinning, too. "Buckle up. We're off to the beach."

And we were, cruising slow down the back roads to the coast, thirty minutes away. Just enough wind came into the car to keep the mosquitoes from settling on us. The dark hid my nervousness at being with Alane. It hid our differences. It made us almost the same.

"I can't believe you are driving," Alane said, her blanket in a pile on the seat between us. She threw her head back and laughed. "My mother would poop a brick if she knew I was out here. She never lets me do a thing. She's too worried."

"Mine too," I said. "I mean, the pooping-a-brick part. This car is my momma's baby. Besides me." I steered with just one hand because I knew it looked cool, but I kept to just under the speed limit. I wasn't too worried about meeting up with one of the three cop cars that patrolled Green River. Past our city limits, though, there was a chance of running into the Jacksonville police. I was always super careful.

"You have the most nerve of anyone I know," Alane said.

I gawked at her. "No, I don't. Shy people don't have nerve, do they?"

"Are you kidding me? Do you know anyone else our age who would do this?"

"No, I guess not." Something like warmth filled me up inside. Driving to the beach at night *was* kind of brave. And *I* was doing it. I'd never thought of it that way before. "There's nothing to it," I said.

We saw only an occasional night driver. Any cars that came up from behind passed us because I was going so slow.

Alane shook her head. "Mom, if you could see me now." Then she reached over to the radio and flicked it on. The whining guitar sound of country music filled the air.

"Country?" Alane said. "Can I change it?"

I shrugged. "If you want."

It took her a second to find a song I'd heard the kids from school listening to. She turned up the volume so loud I could feel the vibration through the steering wheel. The singer started hollering and Alane hollered right along with him.

We were on a clear stretch of road close to the beach, with Alane yelling her head off and me tapping the brake to the rhythm of the music, when it hit me that I wasn't worried about talking to Alane anymore. I'm not sure if it was her awful singing or her wanting to go along on an adventure with me that did it. But I felt good, and not shy at all.

I kept thinking about how Alane had said I was brave. My heart warmed to the idea. And when I pulled to a stop this side of a sand dune and turned the motor off, my ears still pounded with the sound of her crazy music.

chapter 15

Smell that," Alane said, breathing in the salty air. I rolled up the windows to keep the sand fleas out of the car and slipped on my shoes.

In slow motion Alane opened the door. "Let's go," she said, peering at me in the dim glow of the dome light.

I love the beach. I wasted not even a second scooting out of the car and scrambling up and over a low dune. The waves sloshed in against the shore. I could taste the air and smell the wet sand.

"This has got to be," I said to Alane, "one of my very most favoritest places. If you want to get wet, put your shoes here with mine." It felt great saying this to a friend.

She didn't answer.

I looked over my shoulder. Alane was nowhere to be seen. "Alane?" I shouted. And then I saw her wigged head bob up over the top of the sand dune. She moved slower than a roly-poly.

"Need help?" I said, walking back up the dune.

She nodded. "Yeah. I keep forgetting I can't do what everyone else in the world can."

I reached out a hand, steadying Alane as she climbed. She stumbled a little, but she was so light it was easy for me to keep her from falling. "This sand is too dry and shifty," she said. "I'll be okay on the shoreline." She was drawing in deep breaths of air. Her fingers squeezed my wrist.

"Take your time," I said. "We got until your momma gets up in the morning."

Alane looked at me right in the eyes and smiled.

Together we slid down the dune and walked to the edge of the ocean. The moon reflected on the wet sand. The water looked black and scary like in *Jaws*, that old shark movie, and the sea foam kept rolling in and popping near our feet.

It was weird. In all my time talking to Great-Granny Dorothy Lu Lu, I never felt as close to her as I did at that moment with Alane right there beside me.

If she hadn't died, Great-Granny Dorothy Lu Lu would have been close to sixty now. Maybe she would have run off to the beach with me like Alane had.

So it wasn't like it was just me and Alane out there with the water and the moon and the sand fleas.

No, Great-Granny Dorothy Lu Lu was there, too. Keeping an eye on us. Letting me know she was near.

"Can you swim?" I asked Alane after a while. I knew Great-Granny Dorothy Lu Lu could. Not that that had helped her any. She did drown, after all.

A warm breeze blew between us.

"I can swim," Alane said. "But I better not. That water looks too powerful for me."

I stepped down to the edge of the ocean and let the waves wash over my toes. I looked out at the water, the way the moon looked out on the waves. In three or four steps I could dive away from shore and just start swimming. That was one thing I could do. Swim.

The moon iced the waves with a shimmery light. "I could hold on to you," I said.

"I'm not strong," Alane said. "I can't use my legs well."

"We don't have to go deep."

Alane seemed to speak to herself then, her voice low. "It's been so long." She took an uncertain step into the water.

"You're not taking off your shoes?"

She shook her head. Then she grasped my arm and together we started into the ocean. We walked until the water was almost up to Alane's knees.

"It's been so long," Alane said again, and when I looked at her, she was crying. I pretended not to see.

"Let's go a little deeper," she said.

"All right."

We edged our way into the water, the strong waves slapping at our legs. Alane was so tiny, so short, I could have scooped her up and carried her. Even her grip on my arm was frail.

"I'm kneeling," she said, and just like that she plopped down into the water. I squatted beside her. The waves broke a few feet in front of us and rushed forward, white and foamy.

"She never lets me do anything," Alane said. "Not a single thing."

"Who?" I dunked lower, getting my hair wet up to my ears. The water was still summer warm. Something brushed against my hand. I thought about a shark or a Portuguese Man-of-War, then decided not to worry. Great-Granny Dorothy Lu Lu was watching over us tonight. We'd be safe.

"My mother." Alane looked out at the ocean again. A wave buoyed us up, then rushed to shore. "She's always so worried. Poor thing. I feel sorry for her."

I just listened. We were close enough that our shoulders touched.

"Whenever I ask her if I can do something exciting, like ride a roller coaster, she freaks out. 'You might have a heart attack,' she says. Or 'Do you know how I'd feel if you had a stroke?' I try to calm her down and tell her things will be okay. Then she starts all that weeping. I hate it when she cries." Alane sighed. "Don't you just hate it when your mom cries?"

I shrugged. "She doesn't very often. There's not a lot for her to bawl about."

Alane nodded—or else a wave bobbed her up and down. "My mother has everything to cry about. She has me. And my dad, of course. My dad's cool, though."

We were both quiet a minute.

"It's not her fault," Alane said. "Progeria is so rare that only a few kids in the whole world have it at one time. By the time I turned two my mom and dad suspected something was wrong. After the doctors told them what was wrong with me, they decided not to take another chance at bringing more kids into the world."

I didn't know what to say. I bet even Grandma would be speechless. Momma, too, who always has a comment about everything.

"It's like my mother's just waiting for me to keel over and die. She's so scared she won't let me do anything. If she knew about this..."

"Should we go back?" I dug my toes into the sand, holding myself steady.

"Are you kidding? No way! I haven't been to the beach in ages."

"I guess I can't hardly blame your momma," I said, "for being so worried." I took a deep breath. "You couldn't die out here, could you?"

Alane's head tilted to one side, like she was thinking. "Yeah, I guess so."

I struggled to my feet. "Then we have to leave. Right now."

"We're fine," Alane said. "I'm fine." She grinned. "I promise I don't feel a stroke or a heart attack coming on. I got another good year or two in me."

I knelt back into the water beside her. My lips were tingly from worry.

"If I feel like I'm going to croak, I'll tell you in plenty of time for you to get me home."

"Oh," I said. Was she kidding me? "Thanks."

Alane was quiet a moment. "Do you ever wonder what's it like to die, Beauty?"

A wave splashed me and I tasted salt. "I guess so," I said. "I think about when my great-grandmother died. Sometimes I wonder if there's anything waiting for us, or if there's just nothing."

The moon broke out from behind a few clouds, throwing its creamy light over the water.

"It's a little scary to think about," Alane said. "But everybody's going to die. Some of us sooner than others."

"Well, *I'm* not dying," I said. "Not anytime soon, anyway. And neither are you. Let's just be friends and that's it. No croaking, okay?"

"Okay," Alane said. And for a while the two of us sat in the water like fishing bobs, the smell of the water and sand and salt all around us. A breeze blew hard, kicking up the sand on the beach.

"I'm kinda cold," I said. "Are you?"

Alane nodded. "Yeah. But I have my blanket in the car."

We hurried out of the water together, me helping her along. I could feel the gritty sand between our hands and hear Alane's hard breathing. But she never stopped smiling, all the way to Momma's car.

chapter 16

While Alane snuggled up in her blanket, I turned the heater on high and backed the car along the sandy strip that had led us to these dunes. The clock on the dashboard read 2:13 in tiny blue block numbers. The radio music rocked the air. I turned it down some.

The headlights beamed out over the flat Florida land. It was like looking out at nothing, just a dark horizon with trees here and there.

Back out on the road, I glanced at Alane. She had the blanket pulled to her nose. Only her wig and glasses showed. I could hear her teeth chattering.

"Want to drive?" I ask. *Where had that come from?*

Alane's mouth dropped open. "Me? Really? Are you sure?"

"As long as we're on back roads, I don't see why not." I looked ahead of us. Out in the distance I could see moths flitting through the headlight beams.

"I *so* want to," Alane said.

I stopped the car. "Okay." I jumped out and ran to Alane's side. "Slide over then," I said.

She did, leaving her blanket behind. I folded it up on the car seat for her to sit on, so she could sit up higher. With the automatic seat adjustor, I moved Alane close enough for her feet to reach the gas pedal and the brake and helped her with her seat belt. She still could barely see over the steering wheel. The air in the car was steamy and smelled of the beach. After I dropped Alane off, I'd have to roll the windows down to air it out. I couldn't have Momma finding out about my nighttime adventures.

I flipped on the defroster and fastened my seat belt. "That's the brake, and that's the gas. Be real slow pushing on 'em, and you'll be fine. As far as I can tell that's the one thing that matters in night driving. Oh yeah, and not getting caught. So don't speed."

Alane was a natural. I got a slight whiplash from her braking too hard and gunning the gas. It was no worse than what I got when *I* was learning to drive. The way I see it, there are always gonna be neck injuries with beginning drivers.

I only had to scream "Watch it!" three times and "Stop now, please!" twice. What better first-time driving record is there than that? Alane was doing terrific. And we were both getting a good laugh out of it.

Down the road we went, at thirty-five miles an hour. There

were no street lamps now, just the moon to show our way and, of course, the headlights on the car. So I think that's why it took a moment for us to notice the thing in the road.

"What is that?" Alane said, stomping on the brakes. My hands slapped at the dashboard. Thank goodness I had my seat belt on, or I might have smacked into the windshield.

"Sorry," she said.

I don't think Alane had bounced at all. Her seat was pulled as close to the steering wheel as possible.

"That's okay. You're doing good." I squinted through the windshield. There *was* something standing in the middle of the road. "I'm not sure *what* that is. A pig, maybe? Let's go a little closer."

Alane let up on the brakes and the car crept forward a few yards. "It *is* a pig," she said.

"That looks like a boar. Florida's full of 'em." It was still pretty far away, but I could see its curved tusks. "They sure are ugly, aren't they?

It was huge. Like a cow almost, but low to the ground. It was covered with bristly hair. And it had little piggy eyes. "Let's try to go around it," I said. "Looking at that thing gives me the shivers." The car inched forward. The hairy, tusked creature stood its ground, glaring into our headlights.

"Oh my gosh," Alane said, "it's staring at us. Look at those nasty, beady eyes." She stopped the car again.

"I know," I said. The thing could have starred in a horror

98

movie. Red eyes and all. I didn't want to keep looking at it, but I had to.

The animal took a step. Alane held onto the steering wheel with one hand. I leaned over and grabbed the other one. Her fingers felt a little twisted under mine, but her skin was soft.

"It's coming toward us," Alane whispered. "Like it's stalking us."

The thing seemed to paw at the road, then it lowered its head.

"Lock the doors," I said.

The killer boar took another step toward us.

"Hit the lock button," I said. "Quick. It's on the arm panel."

As Alane fumbled for the button, the car eased forward again.

"Stop!" I shouted.

"Stinking heck!" Alane hit the brake pedal with her foot.

The boar-pig let out a snort and began to trot. "He's coming!" Alane shrieked. "What should we do?"

"Lock the doors," I said. "Then throw the car into reverse."

"I can't," Alane said.

The boar sped up, heading straight for us. If it had stood on its hind legs, opened the door, and beat us both up, I wouldn't have been any more surprised than when it charged. "Back up!" I shouted. "Put it in *R!* Put it in *R!*"

Somehow Alane got the car in reverse. But she wasn't as good at driving backward as she had been at driving forward.

She zigzagged into the opposite lane, then zigzagged the other way. The tires squealed.

"You gotta look in the mirror!" I shouted. I glanced out the back window, but I couldn't see a thing. And to tell the truth, I haven't spent that much time in reverse. Going forward has always been the best driving plan for me.

"I can't do this!" Alane shouted.

"Stop!" I was screaming now. We had zigged across the lane again. On this side of the road was a ditch. A deep ditch.

"Stop!"

Alane slammed on the brakes and I lurched against the back of the seat. "Did we lose him?" she asked, putting the car in park. I could see her hands were shaking.

I squeezed my eyes shut. "I think so," I said.

That's when I heard the *bump*. It came from my side of the car. I peered out the window into the darkness. The wild boar stood there now, staring at me.

"He's over here," I said in a pretty loud voice.

Alane screamed and put on the gas. Good thing for us the car was in park or we would have ended up in the ditch. Or maybe we would have leapt over it.

I heard terrible scratching noises. "He's gouging up Momma's paint job!" A quick flash popped into my brain of Momma rubbing wax onto her car after she had it painted this baby blue color. My throat tightened. "Momma's going to kill me."

I took a moment to scream a couple of times. Alane joined me. Then I said, "Alane. We gotta get outta here. We can't stay here all night. And we have to be careful. If we wreck this car, that means we're caught."

"Nobody knows we're gone," Alane said peering at me. I noticed her glasses were steamy.

"Not yet," I said.

"So what do I do now?"

"In *slow* motion, with your foot on the *brake*, put the car in *D*."

"All right," Alane said. "*D*." She squinted as she shifted gears. The boar head-butted the car again. Momma was not going to be happy.

"Now go!"

At that moment Alane became an excellent driver. She did just what I said.

The wheels spun in the dirt next to the ditch. Then the car leapt ahead and Alane struggled, twisting the steering wheel this way and that.

"Slow down! Take your foot *off* the gas!"

Alane did.

The car slowed.

I looked behind us. The boar was trotting down the road in the opposite direction from where we were headed.

"He's gone," I said.

"Oh my gosh," Alane said. "Do you mind taking over the wheel again?

We switched places, and I eased the car back onto the road. We laughed the whole drive home, even though Momma was still going to kill me. I didn't care. Not *that* much.

I had found a friend at last.

chapter 17

We invited Alane over Sunday night for dinner. I met her at the front door and whispered, "Be prepared." Before I had time to explain, in came Momma and Grandma and Jamie.

"Mr. Borget," Alane said, all surprised.

"Hello, Alane," he said. He grinned like nothing else in the world mattered more than seeing Alane at the house with my family. "I'm so glad you're here."

"Thank you, Mr. Borget. I'm glad to be here, too."

Alane said to me in a low voice, "Is *he* what I'm supposed to be prepared for?"

I shook my head and then Grandma and Momma both swooped down on Alane at once. "It's nice to meet you, Alane," Momma said, and Grandma added, "We just love it when we have company." Then Jamie said, "Beauty's mother is an awesome cook." And Momma said, "Oh, Jamie," and slapped at his shoulder. I mean it, she actually *slapped* at him in a little girl sort of way. When Jamie kissed Momma on the cheek, Alane gave me the old raised-eyebrow look. I shook my head again.

"I hope you have fun here," Grandma said. I would have said, "How can Alane have fun when we're still standing in the front hall?" but I wasn't able to get a word in edgewise. Then Jamie said to Momma and Grandma, "Alane is a very good writer." And Grandma said, "Is that so?" And Momma said, "Beauty writes words to songs, don't you, honey?" And I would have answered but I didn't even get to sniff in a bit of air before Grandma said, "Maybe some day you could read us something you wrote, Alane."

Grandma herded us all down the hall to the dining room, where a feast awaited Alane Shriver, honored guest in the McElwrath home.

"Have a seat, Alane," Momma said, pointing to the chair next to mine. "In the place of honor." Overhead, the ceiling fan swirled. Outside the wall of open windows, a breeze moved through the bushes and trees with the promise of a coming storm.

I plopped down next to Alane.

"Thank you for letting me come over," Alane said. Her black wig hair was pulled back in a ponytail, and she wore a pair of blue jeans and a shirt that matched the color of her eyes. You couldn't tell that she'd been at the beach the night before

or that she'd ever driven a vehicle that was attacked by a wild
animal. She smiled around the table. Everyone smiled back.

"We love having you," Momma said. "And it was real nice
to talk to your momma on the phone this afternoon."

"What?" Alane said. Then she shook her head. "Oh, man.
I hate it when my mother does that."

"Does what?" Jamie said.

"Calls ahead." Alane shook out her napkin and laid it in her
lap. "She worries a lot, so she checks out everything I do. You
know. Dangerous things like having dinner with friends."

Grandma and Momma and Jamie all laughed.

"Well, she doesn't need to be worried," I said. "Nothing
ever happens around here."

"Oh, Beauty," Momma said. "It's a momma's duty to worry.
Right, Mommy?"

Grandma nodded. "Sure is."

"This is my first visit to a friend's house in a long time,"
Alane said.

"Well, that makes us even," I said. "Because I hardly ever
have friends over."

Grandma tapped her water glass with her knife. "Attention,
attention," she said. "Let's get this show on the road. I've been
working myself to the nub and I am starving to death."

"Hold your horses, Mommy," Momma said. "We have company, you know."

"I worked in the yard all afternoon," Grandma said. "I don't think I can last another minute without eating. I'm famished."

Alane whispered to me behind her napkin, "I see what you mean."

"What I mean about what?"

"About being prepared," Alane said. She gave me another raised-eyebrow look and gestured to Grandma.

"Oh," I said. "That's not what I meant, either."

"Time for grace," Grandma announced, bowing her head. Last I saw before I bowed *my* head was Alane's wide-open eyes, staring at Grandma.

"Bless this food and all who partake of it," Grandma said. "Now, let's eat." She and Momma and Jamie started chatting and passing around the serving dishes.

"Was that it? Was that what I should be prepared for?" Alane said, whispering behind her napkin. "A fast-food prayer?"

I shook my head and took a piece of fried catfish. "Nope. That's just one of the things you have to get used to if you want to eat with my family."

"No problem," Alane said. "If I get to visit, I'll do things the way you do them. What should I be prepared for, then?"

"Shhh. You'll know," I said. "It's gonna start any minute." Then I passed her the hush puppies while I dished out fruit salad for myself. All was quiet except for the click of silverware against the plates.

"I'm thinking of calling the police," Momma said.

"Because this food is so tasty it should be against the law?" Jamie said.

"Bad joke," I said and Alane giggled.

Momma gave him a smile and I thought she might lean over and kiss him again. I looked away, just in case.

"I think that's a little extreme, Nina, don't you?" Grandma said.

"I agree with you, Grandma," I said. "Just because Jamie said something corny does not mean that he should be arrested."

"Ha ha, Beauty," Jamie said. He made a face at me.

"No, Mommy, I do not think it's too much," Momma said. "I have been invaded. *And* tampered with."

"Momma," I said. "Don't you think we should talk about something that all of us would be interested in? Something even me and Alane might want to hear? Like science projects or global warming?"

"No, not yet," Momma said. "First this. Then that." She looked at Alane. "I'm sorry, sweetie," she said. "But something unimaginable has happened."

Don't ask. I hoped my brain waves were reaching Alane. *Don't ask.*

"What?" Alane said to Momma.

I grimaced, then set to eating. The dam had been opened. We were in for a flood.

"This morning"—Momma used her fork to gesture her

concern at Alane and me, then at Grandma and Jamie—"when I went to drive to work..."

Alane gasped and went a little pale.

"...I found that vandals had vandalized my car."

Momma had been talking about what she called "the car incident" and "vandals" ever since she'd come home from Dickie's.

I was guilty of taking the car, yes. But how was I to know a boar would show up and attack Ringo? That had not been in my plans for the evening.

"Someone stole my car and took it to the beach. There was sand all over the floor. On both sides—you know, driver's side and passenger's. Like whoever used my car had picked up a friend."

Momma, I could see, was winding up to tell Alane the whole thing.

"But worse than that, they scratched up the side of the car in a most unusual way." Momma looked around the room at all of us. "Did I tell you Dickie said he couldn't figure out what had done that gouging?"

"Yes, Momma," I said. "Several times already." I buttered my roll. "Act normal," I said to Alane under my breath.

"Is this—?"

I shook my head.

Momma turned to Grandma. "Okay, Mommy. From this point on we *must* lock up the house and the garage."

"You don't lock the house?" Jamie asked. "Or your car?"

"Of course not," Grandma said. "Why should we? We live in the middle of nowhere. And we know most of the people around here by heart. Not one of our friends would have..."

Grandma paused and Momma said, "Messed with."

"That's right," Grandma said. "Nobody would have *messed with* Nina's car. They know how she loves it."

"So true," Momma said. She shook her head all sad-like and her blond hair shimmered in the evening light. "Anybody who knows me knows how I baby that car."

"She does love that car," I said to Alane.

Alane nodded.

"No one in the world who knows me would have messed with Ringo," Momma said.

Alane's eyes opened wide. "Ringo?"

Momma nodded. "That's my car's name."

"Even if you trust your neighbors," Jamie said, "you still should lock up. It's a dangerous world out there." Now he looked worried.

"You are right," Momma said. "I can see that now." She made a quick sweeping gesture around the table with her knife. "I know this wasn't done by anyone I know. An outsider did it. Probably from another city." Her eyes fixed on me for a moment. I looked away.

"Someone," Grandma said, "from Ocala."

Jamie laughed and put his fork and knife down with a

clatter. "Okay, honey," he said to Momma. "Are you telling me you have no idea at all who did this?"

"I'm telling you," Momma said, leaning over against Jamie's shoulder, "that this was the work of an outsider."

Jamie looked at me first and then at Alane. Alane let out another little gasp. He knew. And he knew we knew.

"*That*," I whispered to my friend, "is what you should be prepared for."

chapter 18

Jamie pulled Alane and me over before class began Monday morning. "So," he said, grinning, "I see you two have become accomplices."

"What ever do you mean, Mr. Borget?" Alane said. She looked at him all innocent-like. And believe me, a seventy-five-year-old sixth grader can look innocent. She cocked her head to the side. Her lips turned down just a tiny bit. She didn't even blush or blink.

He gazed at us. "Come on, Alane, Beauty," he said. "You're going to have to come clean sooner or later."

"Huh?" I said. My intentions had been to follow the plan Alane and I had come up with the night before. Talk, but say nothing. I'm not so great at that. Whenever I do talk to people, I usually tell all.

"You know what I mean," Jamie said. "Taking care of that car is almost as important to your mother as opening a restaurant.

And not just that, Beauty. Driving alone at night is a pretty dangerous thing. It's years before you can even get a learner's license. "

"I know," I said.

"And anyone with eyes could see that that was the work of two little kids. The tiny footprints were one dead giveaway."

"We are not little kids," I said.

"Shhh," Alane said. "Give nothing away to the enemy." She said this right in my face. I could smell her spearmint gum.

Alane linked arms with me. "Mr. Borget," she said, "my client cannot talk at this time." Then the two of us swung around like square-dancing partners and headed into the classroom. But not before I heard Jamie say, "I don't approve of illegal driving, Beauty, but good for you both."

And it *was* good for us both. Because we had each other.

I know, I know. The whole thing sounds dumb, but I liked Alane. Great-Granny Dorothy Lu Lu and her "pretty is" motto was right on. It didn't matter what Alane looked like. It was how she was on the inside. School would be easier now.

And harder, too. I could see that when we walked into the classroom.

Dolly leaned over to Maria and whispered in her ear, then Maria turned back and said something to Chalice. A couple of boys elbowed each other. Cody raised his eyebrows at us.

So Alane and I were accomplices now. So we shared a

secret. So go sew buttons on your underwear, as my grandma likes to say.

The bell rang and Jamie closed the classroom door. He knew about us driving, but I was pretty sure he wouldn't tell Momma. All I had to do was promise that we wouldn't take Ringo again. And for sure we wouldn't.

Jamie had just told the class to settle down when a note plopped on my desk.

He stood in front of the classroom, waiting. The kids all kept talking, their voices dropping a notch or two.

I stared down at the note. I *never* got notes. Not since third grade. Why would one come now? With slow fingers I opened the paper. My heart felt like it was beating twice as fast as normal.

Thought you were on our *side,* it said.

I felt my face go pale.

"Get out your pre-algebra books and we'll do some fun math," Jamie said.

I looked over my shoulder.

Everyone was digging in their desks for their books.

I stared right toward Chalice, Maria, and Dolly. Not one of them looked up at me. In fact, not one person was paying attention to me. It was like that note came from another planet.

I rolled the paper into a tight ball and took in a deep breath.

Pretty is as pretty diz, I told myself. Why did I care what the rest of them thought? I flipped my math book open.

"Follow along on page 26 as I read the introduction to this unit," our teacher said.

Think of how fun it was last night, I thought. *Think about being at the beach with Alane. Get your mind off the note.* But I couldn't. I couldn't even concentrate on page 26.

Alane had that magnifying glass out again.

I felt a stab of embarrassment. Like somehow it was *me* using it. She hadn't had the magnifying glass when we drove to the ocean. Why did she need it now? Why did she have to use it in front of everyone?

Another note flew over my shoulder and landed in my open book.

Thought you wanted to be one of us.

Again I looked back.

Still no one's eyes met mine. Who had this come from? There was no way Dolly could have hit my desk with it. I've seen her play basketball in school. She never once makes a shot. Same with Maria. And Cody was too far in the back, though he did look my way for an instant when I turned the second time. No one seemed to be paying the slightest attention to me. A tiny hope crept into my brain. Maybe, just maybe, someone was asking me to be a part of their group. My fingers trembled holding the paper. Was it Jim Brady? Or Vickie Finlay?

A sound like ocean waves pounded in my ears.

I faced forward again. Why couldn't I just forget about the stupid notes?

When the bell rang for us to all go to lunch, only Alane turned to me. No note thrower showed up, though I kept an eye out for someone who might be…what? Was this a chance for me to do things with other kids in the class? Did someone want to be my friend? Did someone *really* think I was one of them?

"Ready?" Alane said.

Whoever had written the note would see us talking now. I spoke to Alane, but I didn't look at her.

"Momma said she's packed us something extra good," I said, not letting my lips move. I got up, grabbed the lunch bag, and started toward the door.

"What?" Alane said. "I couldn't hear you, Beauty." She touched my arm with her crooked fingers.

Without meaning to, I flinched. And Alane saw. Her eyes did this funny thing and she drew her hand back, like maybe my arm was the gas burner on Momma's stove.

"So you're done?" she said. "We're not friends anymore?" She dropped her hands to her tiny hips.

We were in the doorway now. The hall was packed with kids going to lunch. Their voices rolled toward me, their laughter, too. I didn't know what to do. Try and find out if someone out there liked me? Or stay here with someone who did?

"Come on, Beauty, tell me," Alane said. "Was it those notes? We have fun a couple of times and then you think someone passing you a note is the friend you were searching for all along?"

I looked down at the floor, knowing Jamie could hear us from his desk near the door. He pulled his own lunch out of a brown paper bag.

"I was just wondering who sent it," I said to Alane. "No one ever gives me notes. I mean, this is one of the only times."

She turned away. "I thought you were different from all the other people. I thought you were a friend that would last more than three days."

"I *am* a friend," I said. But my voice wasn't convincing. Even I could hear that.

Someone from another class passed us in the hall. "Hey, check out that midget," he said, loud enough for everyone to hear. Alane looked at him, then back at me.

I held up my lunch bag. "We've got chicken salad with almonds and stuffed olives..." But even as I said the words, I knew I was hiding behind Momma's lunch. I didn't want to be seen with Alane.

She stared me hard in the eyes. "Beauty," she said. "You know I can't help the way I look. I don't *want* to be this way." Then she turned and headed toward the cafeteria, rocking a little because of the way her hips hurt her.

I lowered the bag and let out a small sigh.

"Beauty?" Jamie called from inside the classroom. His voice was full of disappointment. And I didn't blame him. I also didn't answer him. I just turned the opposite way that Alane had gone and left the school again.

This time I hoped I'd never have to come back.

chapter 19

It turned out Momma's boyfriend was also a tattletale. I know, because even at a jog I didn't get three blocks from school before Momma drove up.

"What're you doing here?" I said.

"I think what you mean to ask is what are *you* doing here." Momma had pulled her long blond hair back into a loose French braid. There was a small smudge of something black and greasy under her left eye.

"That's just what I said." The sun beat down hot. I could feel tears trying to sting their way out of my eyes.

"Don't be a smarty-mouth with me, young lady," Momma said, gripping the steering wheel.

I kept my eyes straight ahead and my feet moving toward home.

Momma swerved across the center line and drove alongside me on the wrong side of the road. It's a good thing Green

River's a small place. Otherwise she'd have been in a head-on collision for sure. It would have been all her fault, too, breaking the law like that.

"Jamie just called me at work."

I rolled my eyes.

"I saw that," Momma said. "Beauty, you are getting ready to tangle with me, and I can tell you right now that you are not going to like it, not one little bit."

I trudged on down the sidewalk. An oncoming pickup truck swept wide around Momma's car. The man inside it waved hello. "Hey, Mr. Pauly," Momma called out in a real nice voice.

"You know," Momma said, the hey–Mr. Pauly voice gone, "that I cannot be running home from my job every two or three minutes to baby-sit you."

I kept walking. Head down. Sun hot.

"And you know I'm working overtime to save so I can open up a little diner."

Old news. Momma's been saving for a diner of her own since I don't know when.

"Every time I have to run home it means extra work to make up for the lost hours."

I kept marching.

"Beauty!"

I stopped short. When it registered on Momma that I'd quit moving, she slammed on the brakes and backed up.

"Beauty McElwrath, what is going on with you?"

I shrugged and stared out over the top of the car. I thought about Alane and me, heading off in the dark toward the beach. I thought about our driving lesson and all the fun we'd had. Then I remembered the look on Alane's face when I jerked my arm away from her hand.

"Get in here and let me take you to lunch." Momma's voice was soft now. Kind, even.

"There's no place good to eat," I said. "Not in this nothing town."

"I see you've got the lunch I packed for you and Alane."

I nodded.

"And I can tell that bag's still full. Doesn't even look like you opened it."

I nodded again.

"I *could* take you back to school. You *could* find your friend and the two of you *could* eat together."

From somewhere came the smell of a just-mowed lawn. I heard a screen door slam. The heat of the sun beat down on me and floated up from the dusty sidewalk under my feet.

Momma sat in the car, still and quiet. I squinched my eyes tight against the glare off the Cadillac's shiny hood ornament. "Come on, girl," Momma said. "Come on, Baby."

Something soft and warm moved inside my heart. Still I stood there.

Maybe it was the heat. Or that soft feeling. But something

made me realize, standing there on the side of the road, that no one in my class knew me at all. Not the note thrower. Not Maria or Dolly. Cody had come close, but things had changed with him. Only Alane ever cared enough to find out who I was. And maybe Jamie.

I saw that it didn't matter to the other kids in my class whether I was nice to Alane or mean to her. None of them would be friends with me unless somehow *I* changed. Into what, I wasn't sure. But Alane liked me the way I was. So I was shy. She didn't mind. So I liked to talk with my Great-Granny Dorothy Lu Lu who had been dead for years. Alane was okay with that. I could be a car driver and a secret teller and a song-writer, and that was okay, too.

The problem wasn't the kids in my class. And it wasn't my shyness. Those were just the excuses I always used. The real problem was me. I didn't have a spine.

Sure, I could steal a car at night. I could drive all over Florida if I wanted. Maybe even on a highway. But I couldn't stand up to the kids in my class and stick by the one person who had been a real friend. I had turned my back on Alane just because she was different.

And like Momma had said, it made me just the same as they were.

That thought, baking in my brain there in the afternoon sun, made me a little sick to my stomach. I swallowed twice.

Momma must have seen my swallower working, 'cause she said, "Now that's my girl. Come on, Beauty. I'll drive you back to school."

I hopped into the car, kissed Momma on the face, and said, "Thanks." Then I leaned against the car seat and thought about what to do.

The other kids were just coming back from lunch when I hurried into the classroom. I couldn't think, because thinking might mean I would lose my nerve. And I didn't want to lose my nerve again.

"You're back, Beauty," Jamie said. "Well, I'm glad."

I bet only he and Alane even knew I had left. Right at that moment, I knew I was safe with him here at school.

"Well, I'm glad too," I said.

Alane didn't look up from her book, holding on to that magnifying glass in one tight fist.

Maria and her group sauntered in just as the bell rang.

"Settle down, everybody," Jamie said. "We have work to do. At lunch I was listening to the news and I learned there is a tropical storm forming out over the Atlantic Ocean. Forecasters are saying it could become a hurricane, so I thought a little study on weather systems might be in order."

The classroom started to buzz a bit.

"Let's start our discussion by talking about what factors create a hurricane," Jamie went on.

I raised my hand. What was I doing? *Put your hand down,*

I told myself. *This can wait. You won't lose your nerve.*

"Yes, Beauty," Jamie said. Hearing his voice gave me courage.

"I have something I'd like to say." My voice didn't come out all the way, so I said it again, louder. "Mr. Borget, I have something to say."

"Okay."

Somebody in the back of the room said something, but I couldn't hear what it was. Another kid laughed.

I stood up and stared at the lunch bag I still held in my hands. The top of it was worn and crumpled where I had gripped it so hard.

"I just want to say, first off, I'm sorry I was such a dummy." My voice sounded small again, like maybe I was talking to the sandwiches Momma had prepared. I cleared my throat. "I'm sorry, Alane."

From the corner of my eye, I saw her move in her chair. Was she looking at me? Ignoring me?

Everyone in the class was dead quiet. All I could hear was the clock and the buzz of the fluorescent lights. I kept on talking. "I'm sorry that I cared about what anyone thinks about you." Somebody out in the hall sneezed. "My Great-Granny Dorothy Lu Lu used to say, 'Pretty is as pretty diz.'"

"Pretty what?" a girl whispered. I think it was Vickie Finlay, but I wasn't looking at anything now but the dingy turquoise floor.

"She meant it doesn't matter what you look like, it matters what you do. You just have to be nice. Act nice. Treat people good. And all my life my momma and grandma have been telling me to do that. They've told me if I was good to people, they'd be good to me. And I've done what they said."

I took a big breath, but something the size of a golf ball sat in my throat. It made me sound a little wheezy.

"My last few years going to school here in Green River, I've tried to be nice, but most people have just ignored me. Or else they've been straight out mean. So I started not to believe what my great-grandma said. Then you came to this school, Alane, and I treated you the same way I've been treated all along here. I'm sorry. If you'll still be my friend, I'll never think such dumb thoughts again."

Alane didn't even hesitate. "Of course, Beauty," she said.

"Okay, I'm done," I said to Jamie as I sat down. I had to take real deep breaths to make the tears go away.

"Good for you, Beauty," he said. He turned his attention to the classroom. "Now who remembers the name of the most devastating hurricane in U.S. history?"

chapter
20

S o then what happened?" Alane sat next to me, looking into the river, her legs swinging back and forth. "I don't remember anything from that day, of course," I said. "I was pretty young."

It was a bright, sunny Saturday. The river trickled along in some places and pooled in others, looking all golden like Grandma's topaz ring when the sun shines on it. And to make the weekend even better, Alane and I had had our first sleepover at my house. Alane's momma had called and talked to my momma, giving all kinds of directions and advice and instructions. She'd even called back at 10:30 in the p.m. to see if Alane had gone to bed yet. Sure, we were in bed by 10:30. Good thing she didn't ask if we were asleep.

We'd talked long into the night, with me telling her more about the McElwrath family and our motto and how it near 'bout drives me crazy. Alane had waked me up early, insisting that she felt good enough to take a walk before breakfast. Now we sat at Great-Granny Dorothy Lu Lu's drowning place, listening to the river.

"Just tell me the story the way you've heard it," Alane said.

A red-winged blackbird flew past and landed on the tangle of roots just downstream from us. I heard a dog barking from somewhere—maybe one of Cody's hunting dogs. A butterfly whispered over a small patch of wild clover.

"Okay." I took in a breath of fresh morning air and broke a twig off a tree. "It was late spring and there'd been an unseasonable amount of rainfall that year," I said. "Great-Granny Dorothy Lu Lu and Grandma and Momma and me had been cooped up in the house for weeks. At least that's the way Momma tells it."

"Okay, so then what?" Alane said.

"So we'd been in the house a forever, waiting out the storms. And on the first dry day the three of them decided I needed to get out of the house, on account of I'd been shut in for so long."

Alane looked at me wide-eyed. "You mean, they all came out here because of you?"

I'd never thought of it quite that way. "Yeah, I guess so."

"Okay. Keep going."

I stared at the stream and broke up the twig, tossing pieces of it one by one into the slow-moving water. The smell of late summer flowers blew past on a light breeze. "So we brought lunch. Momma was a wonderful cook even then."

Alane nodded.

"The water was high. Really high. To hear Momma tell it, the river spilled out over the banks. Came all the way past where we're sitting now."

"Wow," Alane said.

"So they were eating and talking and stuff. And all the sudden Great-Granny Dorothy Lu Lu saw I had wandered off."

Alane put her gnarled fingers to her cheeks. "Then what?" Her voice was breathy. From somewhere a mockingbird sang out.

"Well, they started looking for me. One of them said something about the river and they all started running upstream. And sure enough..."

"You were right there, near the water."

"Right. And they called for me. And I ran from them. Laughing. Like we were playing or something."

"And you fell in?" Alane would be a great book writer. It was like she knew the story better than me.

"How did you know that happened?" I asked.

Alane shrugged. "I guessed. Keep going."

I felt a little uneasy. No one outside my family knew this story. At least, not that I knew of. But still I went on. It was almost like I had to get the story out of my head and examine it. Poke it with a stick.

"You fell in, right, Beauty?"

"Yeah, I fell in." Momma had only told me the story a couple of times, but it was here that she would start to cry. Weep, really. You know, where tears run down your face and you keep on talking. For some reason, I felt all teary eyed now, too. "To hear Momma tell it, I went up and down in the water like a red-and-white bobber on an old cane fishing pole. And Great-Granny Dorothy Lu Lu, she didn't even hesitate. Just leapt right in the churning, bubbling water."

Alane wiped at her eye with one hand. Her glasses sat in her lap and caught the glimmer of the morning sun. "And she saved you, huh?"

"Maybe I should stop if you're gonna cry like that."

Alane shook her head. She sniffed big. "It's such a great story. I always cry at great stories. It's my nature. It's what makes me a writer. I always put sad stuff in my stories. Keep going."

"Okay then," I said. "She jumped in the water behind me. Momma and Grandma were screaming their faces off. Momma says when Great-Granny Dorothy Lu Lu jumped into the river that I just turned to her and bobbed right into her arms."

By now Alane had the sub-subs. You know, that place in crying where you're sobbing and grabbing air in little chugs.

"I wrapped my arms around my great-grandmother's neck"—the tears were building up in my eyes, too—"and we were being dragged downriver and Momma and Grandma were running alongside us, trying to get us out, but there just wasn't a way and I was holding tight to Great-Granny Dorothy Lu Lu's neck and everybody was screaming but Great-Granny Dorothy Lu Lu. She was fighting for our very lives. At one point my grandmother got almost close enough to grab us. 'Maggie,' my great-granny shouted—you know, calling Grandma's name. And somehow she pushed me out of the water, toward the shore. Before she could get a foothold, though, the current grabbed her again and pushed her further into the stream. Grandma held onto me, and Momma kept reaching for my great-grandmother. But the water had her for good. And when they found her, she was caught over there in those tree limbs." I gestured with my head toward the other side of the river.

"Dead?" Alane whispered.

I nodded. "Dead and drowned," I said.

We both were quiet for a while. Then Alane said, "I feel her, though, Beauty. It's like she's right here at the river."

"I know," I said, wiping my nose. "I visit her a lot out here."

Alane blinked at me. I could see tears sitting on her lashes. "You visit her?"

"When I need to." And I sure had needed to come to the river a lot so far this year. But it was weird. Now that I knew Alane, some things didn't seem to matter as much anymore. Like feeling nervous and shy all the time, or having to wear a bra, or worrying about being alone. It's like a lot of things had been taken care of in the small package of this one friend.

"Your Great-Granny Dorothy Lu Lu was smart and brave," Alane said.

"Yeah, she was, wasn't she?"

"Just like you, Beauty. Smart and brave." Alane gazed out over the river. Then she turned to me, all thoughtful. "Would you tell me her story again? It's the saddest thing I've ever heard. I just love it."

"Sure," I said, so I did. And my best friend and I cried and cried until it was time to go home to breakfast.

chapter 21

omma had outdone herself, if that was possible, on the food. She'd made strawberry crepes, the berries fresh from our garden. And she'd stirred up a big pitcher of orange juice, frozen from our trees last year. And the bits of spearmint sprinkled on top of the fresh whipped cream? They came from Grandma's herb garden. We had sausage, too, but we got that from the Winn Dixie. We don't have pigs.

Momma tapped her glass of milk with her spoon. Our milk came from the store, too, though a guy used to give us a gallon or two every once in a while from his very own cows, till Momma stopped dating him.

"I have an announcement to make," she said. She dipped her head a little and peered out at us from under her eyebrows, like she was shy. That'll be the day, when Momma turns shy.

"What's that?" Granny said.

Jamie, who had come for breakfast, too, grinned from ear to ear.

Momma smiled like she'd won the Florida lottery or something. Which would be nice. That would mean a lot of money, which would mean—

Jamie touched Momma's hand and I all of a sudden got this jumpy feeling in my stomach.

"Uh-oh," I said to Alane. My face felt as cold as a Popsicle. Had Jamie asked Momma—?

"This is a wonderful thing," Momma said. "It's going to change our lives forever, I think."

"Well," Grandma said, "get on with it, girl."

Alane pushed at the strawberries on her plate with her fork. Outside the dining room window, a small breeze moved the hibiscus bushes Great-Granny Dorothy Lu Lu had planted years ago.

"If you're not going to say anything, Nina," Grandma said, "then we oughta eat. Honey, this looks delicious and I'm starving. Nobody cooks the way you do." When she cut into her crepe, cream filling with strawberries spilled out on the sunshine-yellow plate. "Mmm, I declare, Nina, honey." Grandma's gardening tan made her face glow. "You do beat all in the kitchen."

"Thank you, Mommy," my mother said. "We..." She paused, then spoke real slow. I gripped my fork. "Jamie and I found..."

Another pause.

"A place."

"What?" I didn't mean to shriek, but I know I must have because Alane clapped her hands over her ears. Good thing she wasn't holding her juice or a sharp knife.

"What do you mean, a Place?" I screeched. "What's wrong with *this* Place?"

First the Kiss and now this.

Momma tipped her head sideways a little. Alane tugged at my elbow. That's when I realized I was standing with a strawberry stuck to the end of my fork, pointing it at Jamie.

"Are you getting a place of your own?" Now my voice had gone all squeaky. "For the two of you? To get married in? And to move away from here in?"

"What?" Grandma started to get all excited. "You're getting married? You're getting *married?*" She slapped her bare feet on the wooden floor. "I am so proud of you. You know I am. I am so proud of both of you." Grandma pointed at them with both hands—one holding *her* fork, the other holding a glass of milk.

Jamie cleared his throat. The breeze from the ceiling fan ruffled his hair. "Beauty...Maggie," he said. "We're not getting married."

"Well," I said, feeling a moment's relief. Then I thought of something else. "I hope you're not planning to live together. That would be pretty awful, if you ask me. It might even be against our religion. If we had a religion, I mean."

Momma wasn't smiling anymore. "Beauty," she said. "Hush."

"I *have* asked your mother to marry me," Jamie said.

I gasped.

So did Alane.

So did Grandma.

"Congratulations," Alane said. Now she grinned. There was a bit of strawberry in her braces.

"No congratulations are in order," Jamie said. "She turned me down."

"What?" Grandma said. "You're *not* getting married?"

That's good, I thought. But I didn't say anything. My heart fluttered back to where it belonged, like a butterfly settling on a flower.

"This announcement making has taken a turn for the worse," Momma said.

Jamie shifted in his chair till he faced Momma. "Marrying me would be taking a turn for the worse?"

"You're *not* getting married?" Grandma said again. Her voice sounded flat now, like an old tire. "Oh. Well. Oh. I guess I got my hopes all up for nothing."

"Me, too," Jamie said.

"Me, too," Alane said.

I didn't say anything. Don't get me wrong. I like Jamie a lot. I just wasn't sure I wanted him in the family as a permanent fixture. Not yet, anyway.

"I wanted to say"—Momma's voice was back to its usual loud self—"that Jamie and I found a place to open a *restaurant*. A place right outside Green River, on the road to the ocean. I quit my job at Dickie's. And I leased the space."

Nobody said anything. The ceiling fan twirled in the air.

"You quit your job?" Grandma said after a long moment, though I was sure she'd heard everything Momma said. *I* had. "You leased a restaurant? You're gonna do it?"

Momma let out a whoop that shook the windowpanes.

I couldn't believe it. So many good things were happening to us.

I had a friend. And Momma's dream was coming true, too.

chapter 22

Right after supper we dropped Alane at her house. "Expect a call from me later," she said as she got out of the car. She carried her backpack in one hand and her pillow in the other.

"All right," I said.

We watched her hobble up to the house.

"Shouldn't we help her?" Grandma asked.

"Nope," I said. "She likes to do things herself."

"She doesn't let that disease stop her, does she?" Jamie said.

"She's fine," I said. "She has arthritis, but other than that she's fine."

Momma looked at me in the rearview mirror. "Beauty, you know that Alane is very sick."

I shrugged. "She doesn't act like it. I think Florida is doing her some good. Maybe it's the humidity."

Grandma patted my hand. "She is a sweet little thing."

Momma beeped goodbye as Alane reached her front door.

"Call me!" I shouted out the window.

"I will." Alane waved and disappeared into her home.

Momma turned in her seat and gave us all a great smile. "Ready?" she said. "Our new life awaits."

Grandma let out a war whoop like what you'd hear in an old cowboy movie. Momma and Jamie whooped, too.

"Eek," I said. "Stop it. You three are embarrassing me. Act your ages, please." Momma put the car in gear and gunned the motor.

An old man coming out of the house right next to Alane's looked up, startled.

"Hello, Mr. Clark," Momma hollered out the car window. "I'm on my way to a new life!"

"Good for you, Nina!" Mr. Clark yelled back. He shook the newspaper he held in the air and took a few steps toward us. I thought he might try to catch a ride with our crazy group.

"Hurry, Momma, let's go," I said. "You're attracting a crowd."

"One man doth not a crowd make," Jamie said.

Huh? Teachers sure can say weird things.

Over the ocean, storm clouds darkened the sky. The eye of the hurricane Jamie had practically promised us in class would be passing south of Green River, but we were still in for some bad weather. Maybe even enough rain to fill the river back behind the house. But now the smell of the town blew around us, hot and dirty. Bits of garbage swirled in the wind.

We traveled in the same direction Alane and I had the Night of the Boar. In fact, we had passed Momma's place coming and going to the beach.

"Here it is," Momma said, pulling up in front of a small diner that had bright blue awnings and two large picture windows. Through the glass I could see several booths, all with dark blue seats, and seven or eight square tables. "This is our ticket to the big time," she said. "The people who own this place have never done anything with it. But now we're in charge. It's ours for a year, with options to buy later if we like running the show."

I got out of the car. "Dew Drop Inn," I read from the sign that hung out over the top of the building like a small banner. "You planning on changing the name, Momma?"

"I'm thinking so," she said, coming to stand beside me. "I considered Tasty Pastry, but we'll serve more than breads here. Then I thought of Just Like Home. That wasn't right, either. But I think I've settled on a name. It's one Jamie came up with."

Grandma clapped and Jamie gave a low bow.

"Well, what is it?" I asked.

"You'll just have to wait and see," Momma said.

I hate it when she acts mysterious like that, but I knew better than to try and get the answer out of her just then.

I peered through the front door that had a Closed sign on it.

"Can I help wait tables?" I asked. "Earn some money?" My breath caused a small circle of steam to appear on the window. I rubbed my finger through it, making an exclamation point for the possible excitement that waited behind the glass.

"I don't see why not," Momma said. "If things go right, we could all work here. If things go right, who knows what changes could happen in our lives?" Momma smiled, then grabbed a tight hold onto Jamie. He kissed the top of her head. I pretended not to notice, which is a hard thing for a noticer like me.

"What are we waiting for?" Grandma asked. Her voice was warm. I could tell she was itching to get inside. "I want to check out the bathrooms. Make sure they're in order."

Momma pulled a set of keys from her jeans pocket. She turned to me. "You open the door the first time, Beauty."

I shook my head. "That's your job, Momma. This is your place." Far off in the distance, lightning slashed at the sky. After a bit, thunder rolled toward us, deep-sounding like a drum.

"I know that," she said, grinning like maybe she had a secret. "But I'm planning on calling it Beauty's Diner. Having you open the door the first time might bring us extra good luck."

"What?" I said. "You're naming your restaurant after *me?*"

"Like I said, Jamie came up with the name," Momma said. "And I took right to it."

"Are you all right with that, Beauty?" he asked.

I threw my arms around Jamie. Then, for luck, I opened the door. And all four of us squeezed into Momma's restaurant— into *Beauty's Diner*—together.

*

Alane called at ten o'clock sharp that evening. "I'm taking my mother's car this time," she said. "I'll be at your house at 1:30 a.m."

"Are you kidding?" I said. Momma and Jamie both looked up from where they sat at the kitchen table, poring over a catalog loaded with things cooks use. I gave them a wave and shielded my mouth with one hand.

"Are you sure?" I said, keeping my voice low. "Is that a good idea?" I looked back over my shoulder. Jamie was watching me. "You've only driven once before," I whispered. "And it's supposed to rain later." Hurricane Louisa had moved closer to the coast of Florida. People south of us were told to board up their houses and leave the area if they were near the ocean. But there were no warnings yet for Green River.

"Right," Alane said, "and once that rain begins, I'm stuck in the house like your family was when you were a baby. If I get out now, we can have a little fun before the hurricane reaches land. My mother will not let me out of her sight. Colds."

140

"Colds?" I said.

"She's worried about me catching a cold. They can make me pretty sick. Just be waiting, okay? Stay up."

"All right then," I said. "See you later."

I hung up the phone and grinned at the wall. Alane would do just fine getting over here. All we had to do was pray for no boars.

chapter 23

The whole house was asleep when I got up and padded down the stairs to the living room. Jamie had left before midnight and Momma had gone to bed singing.

"She's in love," Grandma had said.

Momma sure *acted* like it. But that was something to worry about later. Not right now.

I waited for Alane in the living room, a nightlight shining from the hall. Outside, the moon was the color of new butter, and hidden from time to time by the storm clouds that blew in from the coast. Inside, the dark, familiar shapes of our furniture were solid and comforting. On the wall near the door was my favorite picture of Great-Granny Dorothy Lu Lu, Grandma, Momma, and me. I sat perched on Great-Granny Dorothy Lu Lu's hip. My hands were clasped together, my face wrinkled up in laughter. Momma was watching us. Only Grandma looked out at the camera—even she laughed with the moment.

With the tip of my finger I traced the outline of my great-grandmother and me. "I wish I'd known you better," I whispered to her image. If she could have had a chance to know Alane, to be here for the opening of Beauty's Diner, to share my growing up with me.

The clock in the hall donged the half hour. It was 1:30 a.m. I yawned and looked out the living room window. Alane was coasting down the driveway in her mom's car, with just the parking lights on.

I opened the front door as quiet as I could and stepped out onto the screened-in porch. The air felt like a wet blanket, heavy with the coming storm, making it hard to take a deep breath.

Alane parked the car and in her slow way climbed out from behind the steering wheel. When I started down the stairs, she held up her hand for me to wait. Then she wobbled up to where I stood, her face happy in the patchy moonlight.

"Hi, Beauty," she said. "I didn't have one problem with wild animals."

"Thank goodness," I said. I motioned to the two white Adirondack chairs that seemed to almost glow in the night. "Let's sit out here," I said. "If a breeze comes through, it'll be a little cooler."

"Guess who called me?" she whispered.

"Who? Someone from school?" I whispered back.

She nodded. "I'll say."

"Ryan Harding," I said.

Alane scrunched up her face. "Be realistic."

I thought. It couldn't be. Maybe... "Cody? Dolly?"

"Of course not to both those guesses. Mr. *Borget* called."

"He is so nosy. What in the heck did he want?"

Alane eased herself down into the wooden chair, kicked off her shoes, and tucked her feet up underneath her the best she could. From far away came a flash of lightning and then the boom of thunder.

"I'll tell you the whole thing." She held her arms out for emphasis. "I had just taken Mom's keys from her purse and put them in my pocket when the phone rang. It scared the daylights out of me. I was worried that she could hear the keys jangle from all the way upstairs, let alone the telephone."

"Yeah?"

"I grabbed the phone and looked at the Caller ID. It had *your* number on it, so I thought it was you."

"You mean he called from here? From my house?"

"Yes," Alane said. "He fooled me, too."

"The nerve," I said. "I knew he was spying on us. He *is* nosy."

"So anyway, I answered the phone and said, '1:30 a.m. sharp.' Just like that."

I clapped my hand over my mouth. "No way."

"Yep," Alane said. "And he said, 'Whatever you two do tonight, you be careful.' I'm telling you, Beauty, I screamed right into the receiver. I just wasn't expecting a man's voice from your phone."

"Served him right if you broke his eardrum," I said, grinning. "Served him stinking right. Then what happened?"

"He said, 'Ouch.' And then he said, 'Don't do anything that isn't safe, Miss Shriver.' And I said, 'Like what, Mr. Borget?' And he said, 'Alane, I'm serious. No driving tonight.' And so I said, 'Right,' and hung up." She let out a high, squeaky laugh.

"Shhh," I said.

"I can't believe I screamed in our teacher's ear," Alane said.

"Well, he deserved it," I said. "Impersonating me. Who does he think he is?"

"Your father?" Alane said, still laughing.

That sobered me right up. "I don't think so. Not for a while yet. You heard what my momma said. She's not ready to be married."

Alane leaned toward me. "He's a cool teacher. And he's nice to your mom. And grown-ups need each other. I know my mother needs my father." Alane was quiet a minute, letting the storm interrupt our conversation with a rumble of thunder. "There's nothing like having someone you are close to," she said. "And even though we haven't known each other forever, I feel like we have. Don't you?"

"I do," I said. It was true.

Again lightning crackled.

"I know something we can do," I said, "before the rain comes. It's outside, though. You want to do it?"

"Of course I do."

As quiet as we could, Alane and I walked through the house to the kitchen door, and into the backyard to the huge oak that stood outside my window. The sky was dark with clouds, the moon peeking out a little now and then. On the opposite side of the tree hung a tire swing that Great-Granny Dorothy Lu Lu had put up for Grandma when *she* was a little girl. It had been a few years since I'd climbed up into that old tire. Now, with the storm coming and my best friend standing by me, it seemed the perfect time to try again.

"Wanna swing?"

In the dim light I saw Alane's eyes go wide. "Are you kidding me?"

I had to help her up into the tire. I showed her how to tuck her knees high, how to curl her head away if I decided to jump on and ride, too. The night was quiet except for the hot wind rushing through the leaves and the sizzle of the not-so-distant storm.

"Hold on tight," I said.

"I can't wait," she said. "I've never been in a swing like this before."

"Then we're gonna make this a great ride," I said. I got behind Alane and gave the tire a mighty heave. The rope made a screeching sound.

146

"It hasn't been used in a forever," I said.

Alane swung out under the oak, going high toward the branches because she was so light. I pushed her again. "Until tonight I was thinking I was too old to swing," I said.

"Not me," Alane said. "This is great."

The wind helped me push her. My hair swirled in the air, and leaves blew across the lawn. We got the tire going strong, cutting through the night in a long arc.

"I'm getting on now," I said. "On the count of three, you move a little to the side so I don't kick you in the head." I ran hard, pushing the tire and Alane. Then I jumped high, grabbing the rope as I scrambled to stand on the top of the tire.

The rope let out a groan. Together we soared so high into the leaves I could have grabbed a handful. I had forgotten how fun this was. It was like being free. Back and forth we flew, the rope crying out like it was calling to someone far away.

It was on a backward swing that I heard the snap. I looked into the leaves above and saw the rope crumple toward us, slow-mo like in the movies. Then it went slack in my hands. For a moment I stood on almost nothing, just the air and a bit of rubber. I came free of the swing, bicycling in the air and flapping my arms as I sailed toward the earth. I landed on my knees, jarring my teeth, and fell forward onto my chin. But I never lost sight of Alane. Her hair flew out around her. I watched as she and the tire bounced three times. Then she popped free and fell in a crumpled ball.

Fear surged through me like hot water. I tried to get to my feet, but my knees felt broken, like maybe someone had taken a baseball bat to them. So I crawled, feeling dirt and leaves and grass under my palms. I crawled to where Alane lay, her body a little twisted. The tire had rolled from sight. The wind blew. I could smell the earth.

She was dead. I was sure of it before I got there.

And I had killed her. Without meaning to, of course. Just like Great-Granny Dorothy Lu Lu. I hadn't meant for her to die, either. But it had happened, and all because of me.

"No," I said. I crawled close to Alane's body. "No."

It was then that Alane laughed. Her laugh was so loud, I was sure she'd wake Momma and Grandma from their sleep. And maybe even Great-Granny Dorothy Lu Lu from the dead.

When she caught her breath, she grabbed my hand tight in hers.

"Are you okay?" I said, tears stinging at my eyes. "Alane?" I pulled her into a sitting position.

"I'm fine," she said, laughing through the words. "That was great."

Relief flooded my body.

"I'm putting this adventure in my book," she said.

chapter 24

I t rained hard for a week. And hailed. The wind took down some power lines and school was canceled. For two days we didn't even have a phone. Grandma kept saying we were lucky we were so far north of the eye of the storm. Hurricanes can be deadly.

Of course, Alane couldn't come over. Just as she'd said, her momma was worried that she'd catch a cold.

"For her, Beauty," Momma said, packing up a few of her own pots and pans to take to the restaurant, "a cold can mean pneumonia. And pneumonia is a scary thing."

"Come on, Momma," I said. I was tired of all this fuss when adults talked about Alane and her being, well...old. "Alane's twelve. She's two and half months younger than me. That means she'll die two and a half months after I do when we're both ninety-six. She's not catching pneumonia. We're planning on getting an apartment together when we're eighteen. In Orlando."

Momma nodded at Grandma, who sat at the kitchen table sorting all of Momma's best recipes for the menu at Beauty's Diner. The plan was to open the second Saturday in October, just three weeks from now. I'd already spent a good amount of time practicing waiting tables at home. I was a pretty good waitress, if I do say so myself. "May I take your order, sir?" rolled off my tongue like spit.

Most of the time, though, I waited for the rain to stop. And waited. And waited. After awhile, even reading got to be boring. And my songwriting took a turn for the worse. If nothing's happening, I found, there was nothing to write about. Was Alane having the same problem with her writing?

Alane called once after the phone lines came back up and said she had big plans for us when the weather was good again.

"And what're those?" I sat on my bed in my room, an unopened book beside me.

"The river," Alane said.

"Huh?"

"What better time of year for me to see where Great-Granny Dorothy Lu Lu died? The water will be high, just like that day. The rains will have been falling, just like that day. We could even take a picnic, just like that day."

Why not? Truth was, I'd never been to the river when it was running high. Momma would skin me alive for doing that. The thought was a little scary, and a lot exciting. "Sounds promising," I said.

"And," Alane said, "this is the best part, Beauty. We could have a séance."

"What? Why a séance?"

Alane let out a big breath of air. "Why do you think? To call back the dead, of course."

"Umm, Alane," I said. The thought of seeing the dead was a bit unsettling. I mean, think about it. "Why would we want to do that?"

"Beauty." Alane's voice sounded like she had some teaching to do and I was the one that needed to do the learning. "We won't call back just *any* dead. We'll try and get Great-Granny Dorothy Lu Lu to stop in."

I didn't say anything.

"You've felt her plenty of times, right? You've known she was out there with you. Wouldn't you love to see her one more time?"

"Well, maybe," I said. "If she was the same great-grandma from when I was a baby. But what if she was just bones and, you know, all scary looking and everything?"

Alane laughed. "This isn't a horror movie, Beauty," she said. "This is real life."

I shrugged, even though Alane couldn't see me. "I'll do it if you want to."

"We're on then."

✳

The sun came up bright on Sunday following the storm, with billowy white clouds in the sky. Momma and Grandma and Jamie went their way—to the restaurant. Alane and I went our way, loaded down with food and drink, to find a spot near the river to perform a séance.

"This," Alane said, stepping with care, "is like a jungle adventure movie." We were trudging through our property toward the river. There was a fresh-washed smell to the air.

"Jungle-y until you think of our séance plans. Then it gets witchy."

Alane let out a snort. "There aren't witches at séances," she said. I wasn't so sure about that.

The ground was soggy, like a sponge left too long in dishwater. Behind us, we left a trail of footprints. If there wasn't any grass where we had stepped, our tennis shoe imprints filled up with water. And even though the sun sat up hot and high in the sky, the trees out here were still dark from the rain.

Alane and I walked side by side, making our slow way.

"Yahoo!" I screeched, glad to be in the outside world with my friend. My voice got caught in the trees and only a little of the sound echoed away.

"Whoopee!" Alane hollered. "Yahoodles!"

Happiness bubbled up inside me like water boiling in Momma's pasta pot. I was so glad the rain had stopped before the weekend and hadn't kept on until just in time for us to go back to school.

Alane carried the blanket tucked in front of her like a big belly. I lugged two picnic lunches in brown bags. I had to make them myself because Momma was too busy to help pack an extraordinary we're-finally-out-of-the-house lunch.

I stopped for a second, shifting the two-liter 7UP bottle that I'd filled with milk from under one arm to the other.

"The river's way high," I said.

Alane looked at me. Her glasses caught the sun and I could see the reflection of the oak leaves in them. "How do you know?"

"Listen."

Alane moved her head to the side, like she was trying to get a little closer to the river. All around us was sound. Birds singing, the slight rustle of the wind in the trees. And, not that far away, the call of the rushing water.

"Too bad it's not dark," Alane said. She gave the blanket a little squeeze. "I think calling back the dead is best done in the dark. With lots of candles."

"You might be right." A shiver ran down my neck. "But your momma and mine both would've had an infarction if they'd thought we were coming down here at night. Anyway, it wasn't dark when Great-Granny Dorothy Lu Lu died. It was the middle of the day. Just like now. And I packed a candle like you said. Remember the one shaped like a bear, with its arms out? There's a wick coming out of each hand and the top of the bear's head, too."

"That'll do," Alane said.

We started walking again. In a little bit we reached the open area where Great-Granny Dorothy Lu Lu and Grandma and Momma and me had picnicked so long ago. The grass was shiny and long, the air steamy. Yellow flowers dotted the far side of the field, making it look like an artist had swooped down and touched the tops of the grasses with her paintbrush.

"Isn't this exciting?" Alane said. She flung the blanket out in front of her a few times, holding it by the corners. It flapped out wide, then settled onto the grasses, held up from the damp earth. A few dragonflies darted here and there.

"Séance first thing," she said. "Get the candle ready."

lane set the bear, all three wicks burning, on a smooth patch of ground. The flames seemed almost not there in the daylight.

"You *cannot* tell my mother that we came out here today," she said. "Who knows what she'll do to me if she finds out."

"Right," I said.

"Now I saw this on TV," Alane said. "And I've read books about it, too, so I am pretty sure what to do."

"Okay." There was a giggle sitting in the back of my throat but I knew better than to let it out.

"Join hands," she said, her voice deep and low.

"Yes, ma'am." I used a deep voice, too.

"Beauty," Alane said, her twisted fingers squeezing mine. "Listen. This is dead serious."

"*Dead* serious?" It was getting harder to hold down the giggle.

She dropped my hands, then knit her eyebrows together and glared at me. "This is important to me, Beauty," she whispered. "I've *got* to contact your great-grandmother."

A mockingbird on a branch above us sang a short song and a squirrel chattered in the distance. On the ground, the bear-candle flames flickered as a breeze pushed past us on its way to the river. The sweet smell of cleaned earth was all around.

"Why do you need to contact her?" I said. "I gotta tell you something, Alane. Holding a séance, even at noon-thirty, is scary."

"You're afraid?"

I nodded. "A little." Maybe she'd never seen dead people in movies, but I had. I knew how those zombies walked all stiff-legged, their eyeballs staring, their hands clutching at the living.

"Nothing scary, I promise," Alane said. "It's just that I've got to know what it's like on the other side." Her voice was still low, like maybe she didn't want the woods to know what she thought.

"The other side of what?" I said, checking for I-don't-know-what behind me.

She paused a moment. "I've got to know what it's like to die," Alane said. "I have to know if I should be afraid. I have to see if Great-Granny Dorothy Lu Lu looks happy. I've heard that people who have died before come to get you when it's time. I want to know if that's true. I need to find out who might come for me."

"Why do you need to know that?" I said. My heart thumped cold blood in my throat. "Why? You're fine. You're just fine."

Alane stared down at the candle bear. "A person can never tell when, well, you know...when they're going to die. It's never when you expect it. Even if you do have a fatal disease."

"What do you mean?" The hair on the back of my neck stood up.

"Beauty, look." Alane kept her eyes on mine. "I would have told you sooner, but I wasn't sure if we were good enough friends."

"It's okay, you don't have to tell me anything."

"And then with the school thing, you know, you not liking me at first."

My face felt like a fire-roasted tomato. "I did want to be your friend."

"Well, until you said that pretty-is-as-pretty-does thing—"

"Diz," I said, looking away from Alane. I'll tell you right now, shame is an ugly thing to feel.

"Right. 'Pretty is as pretty diz.' Well, until you said that in class, I didn't know you *were* a true friend. So I just kept quiet about it."

When Momma said Alane was sick...was that for real?

"Beauty, I don't have that much time left to live."

"What?" I was beginning to panic now. "Don't say that, Alane."

157

"Some kids with progeria die around the age of thirteen or so. I mean, I might only have about a year until—"

"Don't *say* that," I said. My face felt numb.

"I have to," Alane said. "You have to know. We're friends now. I have to be honest."

Alane was right. I knew that. I had to hear her out. Even if I didn't want to. Even if it hurt.

"This disease makes me look old on the outside, but it makes me old on the inside, too. I'm like a stinking old woman. My heart is weak." Alane paused. "The doctors told my parents I could have a heart attack or a stroke any minute. And I just want to be prepared. You know, to die. And I think I can be ready here. I mean, maybe this is why we came all the way from Tulsa to Green River. So I could meet you. And your family and Mr. Borget. And Great-Granny Dorothy Lu Lu, too."

"Okay," I said. I took Alane's hands and looked down at the bear candle so she couldn't see my tears. All three flames wavered in the little pools of melted wax. "Okay, then. Let's do it."

I didn't know how to get rid of the lump in my throat. I squeezed my eyes shut and listened to Alane's voice, her normal voice now, as she talked to the dead.

"Great-Granny Dorothy Lu Lu, we are here to call you back from the grave. To feel your presence once again. To ask you questions about what it's like to die."

I sucked in air through my mouth. How could Alane talk about dying? Let alone ask my dead great-grandmother about it?

And then I knew how. And why. She was afraid. Afraid of what was coming.

I'm not sure why, but I started to chant. It just seemed like the right thing to do. "Dor-o-thy-Lu-Lu, Dor-o-thy-Lu-Lu," I sang as Alane called for my great-grandmother. We kept it up for a long minute, the low drumbeat of my chant under Alane's pleading words. Then, without a signal, we both hushed.

Around us the noise had stopped altogether. Not one bird or grasshopper or frog made a sound. Everything was quiet. We waited a good long time for Great-Granny Dorothy Lu Lu, but she didn't show.

Alane dropped my hands. "She isn't coming," she said. "They never come."

The sun slipped behind a cloud and a shadow fell on us. "What do you mean, they never come?"

"I had séances by myself in every city we stopped at between here and Oklahoma. Not one spirit has come to answer my questions."

"Oh." What does a person say to something like that?

"Let's eat lunch," Alane said. The candle flames had flickered out. She lowered herself onto the blanket in slow motion. "My hips are hurting," she said. "Arthritis. It was bad during the storm."

I realized something weird then. My very best friend had more aches and pains than my own grandmother. Alane was *older* than Grandma. Not in years, but in body.

I unpacked peanut butter and guava jelly sandwiches, Oreo cookies, and Twix candy bars. I poured milk from the 7UP bottle into plastic glasses. We ate in silence, Alane staring out over my head, toward the river. And the whole time I thought I might start bawling. Here I'd finally found a friend and she wasn't even going to be around that long.

When she was done eating, Alane said, "Beauty, I really thought I'd see your Great-Granny Dorothy Lu Lu. I really thought she might be different, that she'd tell me what I need to know. What I should expect."

I was quiet a moment, unsure of what to say.

"She could've at least showed up," Alane said, sounding grumpy. "Even if she didn't say anything."

"I'm sorry," I said, and I meant it.

With a great effort, Alane rose to her knees. "Let's go look at the river," she said.

✳

We made our way through the trees until the river was in view. The sight of the water moving so fast, splashing up and over the edge, made my heart thump.

"Would you look at that?" Alane said, hurrying toward the overrun banks.

"Don't get too close," I said. "It's awfully high." Water crashed downstream, churning against the roots of the trees growing near the banks. I felt real fear staring out at that water.

"So do you think she saw something like this that day?"

"Maybe." My voice was no more than a whisper.

"The water just this high? Just this strong?"

"I don't remember. Maybe."

Alane seemed to be hypnotized by the almost-flood. "It's so powerful."

Staring at the rushing water made me dizzy. I wanted to back up, move away from this soggy ground, though I felt sure we were safe here.

Alane looked over at me. "You want to hear something funny?"

I nodded.

"In still water, I move the same as other people. My mom says it's an equalizer. You know. It makes us the same. Except I don't swim very well."

Again I nodded, remembering our trip to the ocean.

"How deep do you think it is?" Alane said.

"Maybe up to my neck," I said. "Maybe a little deeper in places. I can see over the banks when I'm down there trying to catch tadpoles."

"I bet it *was* the same that day." Alane still stared at the water.

"It could have been," I said. It was weird thinking that Great-Granny Dorothy Lu Lu had been swept into a torrent like this one. It was also weird to think of her rescuing me from my own death in this very place. I mean, I'd thought about it plenty before. But I'd never seen the river running this high. The whole thing—the water looking so angry, the image of Great-Granny Dorothy Lu Lu leaping into the water, the thought of me almost drowning—just about took my breath away.

Alane took a slow step forward.

"Don't go any further," I said. "The current's really strong."

"I know." She kept inching toward the edge of the bank until the water lapped at her tennis shoes. She took two more steps, then she stopped and looked back at me. "Beauty," she said. There was a smile on her face—a small one on the edges of her lips. "I can feel her again. I can feel your great-grandmother."

The trees across the water from us hung dark toward the earth, the Spanish moss heavy with rain. Alane plopped down on her butt.

"Alane! What in the heck are you doing?" I couldn't move. "Stop. You're scaring me."

"I just want to dangle my feet." She scooted herself forward until her legs floated out in front of her. Now she was wet to the hip. "Beauty," she said. "I have the best time when I'm with you."

"Come back this way," I said. "I'm not kidding, Alane. Come back." I waded out until I stood a couple of steps behind Alane, my stomach turning somersaults.

She peeked back at me, then kicked her feet. "You are the best friend I've ever had."

It was right then, right with those very words, that the soft earth where Alane sat started to give way.

"Whoa!" she said, her voice coming out a yelp.

"No!" I reached for her, grabbing her shirt at the shoulder. "Oh my gosh, oh my gosh, Alane!" I'm pretty sure she didn't hear a word I said.

"Good catch," she said, laughing.

Then there was a *sloosh* and the ground under Alane slipped away, turning the water dark brown.

chapter 26

should have known better than to step forward. When my foot hit that soft ground, more of it crumbled away. I held onto Alane's shirt, trying to drag her back, but the current was too strong. It pulled Alane into the water, then me.

The cold made me gasp in a sharp, painful breath. *Get out,* I thought. I grabbed at mud with my left hand and hung onto Alane's shirt with my right. If I could just keep us close to the bank, we'd be fine.

Alane let out a cry of fear. I saw her feet sweep out from under her. Then she was under the water, on her back, the toes of her shoes sticking up. She reached out for me, her twisted fingers just missing my face. Digging my feet into the sand, I managed to jerk her above the surface of the water.

I tried to edge toward the bank, but the river pulled both of us out farther. The sound of a far-off train roared in my ears. I slapped at the water with my free arm.

"It can't be over my head," I said to no one.

The current rolled Alane from her back to her stomach, twisting my wrist with the fabric of her shirt. She grabbed at me again, her hands clawing at my shoulders. Then she floated upright and we were more or less steady for an instant. I felt her feet kick at my legs. I dragged us closer to the bank.

Then the sand under my feet gave way, and I was in over my head, looking through the murky, bubbling water. Something powerful and determined was pulling Alane away from me.

I held onto her with both hands now. She clutched at me, too. The water tugged at us both, trying to rip us apart. Trying to carry us away, like it did Great-Granny Dorothy Lu Lu.

I refused to let go of Alane. We stayed together, two girls tangled up in a ball too heavy to float. Finally, my feet touched the sandy river bottom again, and I pushed us up as hard as I could. Our faces broke the surface. It felt like someone shoved me from behind and tried to push us back under the water, tried to keep us down. Alane squeezed her eyes shut. Her glasses were gone.

"Get a breath," I shouted at her. Then I filled my own lungs as full as I could. Under the water we went again. Something dark slid by. At first I thought a wild animal had come to finish us off. Then I realized it was Alane's wig, rushing away with the current.

Oh, Lord, I thought. *Are we ever in big trouble. I have to get us to the bank...*

Impossible. I was having trouble just getting us up for air. How could I make it to the bank of the river pulling Alane?

We bobbed up. I felt Alane's grip lessen a little.

"Hold on." I wanted to yell, but it was all I could do to make any sound at all. My hands were frozen in place. Something hit me in the back of the head.

"Hold on to me, Alane." I pushed her toward the surface, going under the water again. Loose sand hit me in the face, and I could feel it between my teeth. I pushed off the bottom again. For a moment I could see sky. I tried to breathe and sucked in water. Then I lost my footing and we rolled.

A memory came into my head, not a story someone else had told me, but a real memory of my last day with Great-Granny Dorothy Lu Lu. It was just like a movie. The two of us on solid ground at the picnic. Me stepping too close to the edge of the river. Falling. Great-Granny Dorothy Lu Lu, hollering like nothing else. Then she was in the water beside me. The two of us tumbling. Me clutching at her neck. Her nails scratching at my plump arm.

"Keep up in the air, Baby Beauty!" Great-Granny Dorothy Lu Lu had yelled.

I remembered her words as pure as sunlight. And I saw the whole thing in my mind, like I was standing on the bank watching it. Saw us tumbling and slipping. Heard Momma and Grandma screaming out for us, calling our names. Felt that last swirl, the water almost taking me away and Great-Granny

Dorothy Lu Lu saying, "I love you, Beauty..." Then I was on dry ground in my grandmother's arms, and my great-grandmother was gone.

My whole life did not pass in front of my eyes like people say as I held onto Alane. Just that one thing. Just my last moments with my great-grandmother.

Momma, I thought. *Grandma.* And then *Great-Granny Dorothy Lu Lu.*

My feet hit something solid and the force of the water eased some. I backed into whatever it was. My arms seemed to have lost all feeling. With my last bit of strength I shoved us up toward the blue of the leftover sky. Then we were slammed into the roots of the tree that had caught Great-Granny Dorothy Lu Lu all those years before.

I pulled Alane's head up just above the break of the water.

The water pushed us tight against the roots, and we hugged each other. But it was just me hanging onto Alane. She'd gone all loose in my arms.

"Alane," I said.

At first I thought she was dead. But then her eyes fluttered open.

She didn't say anything. Neither did I. We just let the water push us into this snarl of tree roots. Just let it hold us safe in its fury.

"How did you do it?" Alane said. "You kept me up in the air the whole time."

I didn't answer. I just breathed. Hanging there in those roots, I felt like I had run from Green River to Miami and back again even though I knew we hadn't been in the river even a minute. Every part of me shook. My nose and throat burned.

The river was still a wild thing. It kept clawing and grabbing and pulling at us, though after a while it didn't seem as interested.

Alane leaned her head back some, resting against me.

"We can't stay here forever," I said. "We've got to get out of here. Can you hold onto the roots all by yourself?"

She nodded.

"Then I'm climbing out and pulling you up after me."

Alane nodded again.

"Hold tight now," I said.

The water pounded at my back like a bully when I tried to find a foothold. I shook so hard all over, my feet had a hard time not jerking around. My shoes were gone. Somehow I got situated on a low root and started climbing up to the bank.

"Just hold tight," I called when I was away from the water's grasp. "I'm nearly out."

"Okay." Alane sounded miles below.

I dragged myself toward the bank. It seemed to take forever. At last I was able to pull myself up to the trunk of the tree. I reached back for Alane, who clung, eyes closed, on the roots in the cold water.

"Come on," I said. I gripped her wrists and pulled. Finding an occasional toehold in the tree roots, she struggled out of the water. At last I dragged her up beside me. She was barefoot, too. And missing a sock.

Alane crept onto the bank, then lay still on the ground.

I collapsed next to her, making sure she was still breathing. With her wig gone, I could see Alane's head. She *did* have hair, but it was fine, baby hair. I touched her arm, feeling her near-transparent skin.

I started to cry. My tears ran warm down my cheeks. "We almost died," I said. "Like my Great-Granny Dorothy Lu Lu."

Alane opened her eyes. She gave me a little nod, but that was all the movement she made. "I know."

"My momma couldn't have stood that," I said. "Her grandma gone first. Then me. And you. Finding us drowned would have killed her."

"And my mother, too," Alane said.

Now I was bawling. "You *are* going to die, aren't you?" I gasped for air.

Alane didn't even hesitate when she answered me. "Yes," she said.

Rolling onto my stomach, I buried my face in my arms. It just wasn't fair. None of it. Not Great-Granny Dorothy Lu Lu dying, not Alane having to die, too, not me losing my best friends. None of it was fair.

169

The oak leaves over our heads rustled in the wind.

Alane put her hand on my arm. Her voice was low. "It's okay, Beauty. I'm gonna be okay."

I sat up and wiped at my eyes. Sun splashed around us in patches. From somewhere a mockingbird let out a cry. Behind me the river still roared like it was alive.

Alane pushed herself up and leaned against me. "The dead *do* meet us when it's time to go," she said. "They do."

"The séance was a flop," I said. "We couldn't reach Great-Granny Dorothy Lu Lu."

Alane's lips had gone blue and she was shivering. I had to move close to hear her.

"She told me so."

What?

"Great-Granny Dorothy Lu Lu told me not to be afraid. And now I'm not."

I couldn't speak.

"She came," Alane said. "When we were in the water. And we're not alone when we die. She told me so."

I stared at Alane knowing, somehow, that what she said was true. She had seen my great-grandmother for real.

chapter 27

Two Mondays after the accident Momma decided it was time for me to go back to school. She said I'd had a long enough vacation. And she didn't listen to one word of my arguments, even when I told her I didn't think I could do it alone.

"Yes, you can, Beauty," Momma said. "You are a McElwrath and we do what we have to do. Always."

So I headed off to class, knowing that Alane wouldn't be there but that everyone else would. I would be alone again, without my friend.

That morning the whole classroom went silent when I came in. I sat in my desk at the front of the classroom, Alane's chair next to me, empty. Jamie welcomed me back with a "Nice to see you, Beauty," then turned to the rest of the students in the room. "I just wanted you all to know that Alane's pneumonia has cleared up and she's getting better," he said.

Jamie stood silent, his hands clasped in front of him. I remembered how upset he had been when I ran home for help and he had to go back for Alane. I could tell by looking at him now that he cared. Not just about Alane. But about me, too. And everyone else in this classroom, too.

"We could send her more get-well cards," someone said. I looked back. It was Vickie Finlay.

"That's a good idea," said Dolly.

"We'll make some more get-well cards, then," Jamie said.

"I don't think so," I said. All the sudden, I felt angry. None of these kids had tried to be Alane's friend. Not a single one. And now they wanted to send her cards?

"What do you mean, Beauty?" Jamie said.

My shyness gene seemed to have melted away, at least for the moment. My mouth took off without my permission. "No one was ever nice to her. Everybody ignored her. You can't make it up in cards."

Jamie just looked at me.

I glared around the room, my chin up, my eyes squinting mad. "You made fun of her, and when I tried to be her friend, you were even meaner. It's been awful for Alane everywhere she's gone to school. She hoped we would be nice to her. And no one was."

"Not even you, Beauty," Maria said.

"I know that," I said. "But I've tried to make up for being such a jerk."

The class was silent.

Most people didn't look at me. Chalice picked at her finger-nail. Ryan pretended to be interested in his geography book.

The person who surprised me was Dolly. "I'm so sorry, Beauty," she said. Tears rolled down her cheeks. Then she burst out, "I'm sorry I was mean to Alane. And I'm sorry I haven't been nicer to you."

That seemed to loosen the class up some. Don't get me wrong, everyone didn't run up and hug my neck and tell me they wanted to be friends forever. And there were a few snickers. But most of the kids seemed to be sad about Alane. Jamie gave everyone a chance to have their say, and I was surprised to see that in just a couple of weeks, some of my classmates had started to change. And all because of Alane.

On my way to lunch, Jamie stopped me. "You're growing up, Beauty," he said. "Your mother would be proud."

I just gave him a little nod and headed toward the lunch-room. Momma had packed me a great lunch with stuffed cel-ery, homemade clam chowder, and fruit salad with whipped almond topping. I plopped down at the end of a table and tried not to think of Alane. I wouldn't be allowed to see her, accord-ing to her mother, "For some time."

I wasn't allowed to talk to Alane except when her mother let her call, and that wasn't often. Fact is, if Momma hadn't run interference for me, I never would've gotten to talk to Alane again.

"Alane's mother was madder than a hornet for a while there, Beauty," Momma told me. "She called me up after they had to take Alane to the hospital and let me have an earful." Then Momma spent a goodly amount of time giving me what for. Grandma did, too.

Finally I fought back and told them how I felt. Didn't they know I'd already thought of all that good and long on my own? Didn't they realize it was me in that water—again—and with my best friend this time? And couldn't they see that we'd both nearly died—a thought that made my stomach flop with fear every time it came to mind?

Momma and Grandma stopped their fussing then and let me be. In fact, they went all soft. Then my momma called Alane's mother and told her how the whole thing was an accident and how much I missed Alane. And Momma must have said a lot of other stuff, too, 'cause now it seemed they were on the phone more than Alane and I were.

"Hey, can I eat with you?"

I looked up to see Vickie holding her tray, waiting for an answer.

"Sure," I said.

Vickie cleared her throat and said, real fast, like everything coming out of her mouth was one sentence, "Beauty, I wanted to be friends with you and Alane, but I was too shy to say anything. And then once you started hanging out together I thought...well...I just want you to know I'm real sorry about Alane." She sat down.

I looked at Vickie. Her eyes matched her brown hair. "Thanks," I said. And then, "You'll like Alane."

Just saying the words made a lump come up in my throat. Would Vickie have a chance to get to know my best friend?

I didn't get to finish my chowder and fruit salad. People kept coming up to say they were sorry and to ask about what had happened. I didn't tell anyone the truth. I wasn't ready for the whole story to be out. And anyway, how could I explain Great-Granny Dorothy Lu Lu coming back for a visit? Some things are better left unsaid.

Then, on my way into our classroom, Cody stopped me. "Hey," he said, "I'm real sorry about Alane. Is she gonna be okay?"

"Of course she is," I said, pushing past him.

He followed me to my seat.

"And I'm real sorry about not staying your friend over the summer."

"I just got kinda scared or something, Beauty. I guess I was starting to like you and then I...well, I don't know..."

"No problem, Cody," I said.

"You sure?"

"I promise." Maybe Cody won't be the guy I marry, but when he said all that to me it did smooth things over a bit.

✳

Right after school, I headed over to Beauty's Diner. I was getting pretty good at waiting tables—in fact, I hadn't dumped a drink on anyone yet.

Between customers I did my homework at a booth in the back corner, one that let me look out on the road Alane and I had driven down not that long ago. After we'd shooed the last diner out the door, Momma and I went into the kitchen to do a final cleanup.

The restaurant business was hard work, but I hadn't seen Momma this happy since I don't know when. Grandma and Jamie spent their free time helping out, too, but tonight it was just me and Momma.

Momma gave the restaurant kitchen a last look-over. "I think," she said, "we've got it all done. And in record time, too. It's nine thirty." Momma propped her hand on her hip. "You want to visit with Alane for a few minutes tonight?"

I looked at Momma, not quite believing her. "Really?"

"Mrs. Shriver said you could come by as long as it wasn't after ten." Momma ran her hands over her apron.

A careful joy surfaced in my chest. "Of course I want to go," I said. "You know I do." I threw my cleaning rag on top of the pile of dirty tablecloths and napkins that we needed to run through the washer at home.

"Carry the basket to the car, then, and I'll lock up."

I slid the laundry basket in the backseat on the boar side of the car that Momma had repaired not long after mine and Alane's little run-in with Florida wildlife. I breathed in deep, tasting the fall air.

In the distance, the moon was rising, lighting the sky all different shades of blue, including one that matched the booths in Beauty's Diner. I couldn't wait to see Alane.

Momma came outside and locked up. In just a few moments we were on our way to the Shrivers' house. We rolled the windows down to let the October air breeze through Ringo.

"Momma," I said. "There's something I gotta tell you." I stared into the side mirror, watching the telephone poles zip by.

"What's that, Beauty?"

"I took your car out the night it got dented. It was me and Alane. And a wild boar gouged up the side. I'm sorry."

Momma looked at me side-eyed. "Oh, I knew it was you," she said. "I figured that out right away."

"What?" I peeked over at my mother. "How?"

"Well, for one thing, the radio was blasting some kind of crazy screaming music when I got into the car the next morning. And there was white beach sand on the floor, including three perfect footprints. Two were just your size."

Ding dang it!

"So why didn't you say something?" I snuck another glance at my mom. Her long blond hair blew in the wind. She drove with just one hand on the wheel. She'd started letting her nails grow out after all that time working at a gas station and having to keep them short. They were painted a pearly pink.

Momma smiled. "I knew you'd talk to me about it when you were ready. I was just waiting on you." She stopped the car in front of Alane's house. Then she turned and gave me the Old Eyeball. "Now that you've brought it up, don't you be driving ever again without a license. I mean it. It's dangerous, and it is against the law. You hear?"

"Yes, ma'am." I sat still a moment. "Momma?"

"Yeah, Baby?"

My heart thumped at what I was about to say. "So do you think my helping Alane out of the water kind of makes things even?" I couldn't look at her when I asked, so I stared into the dark night, past the street lamp that made the sky seem even darker than it was.

"Makes things even with what, Beauty?"

It took me two tries to get started. "You know," I said at last. "With Great-Granny Dorothy Lu Lu dying. On account of me, I mean. She died because I went near the river. In a way, I killed her. So have I made up for that, helping Alane out of the river?"

"Killed Great-Granny Dorothy Lu Lu?" Momma sounded shocked. "Beauty, that was an accident. You were three years old. You didn't kill her. You weren't nothing but a baby. And there was no way one of us wasn't going in the water that afternoon. We *had* to save you. Great-Granny Dorothy Lu Lu just got there before Mommy or I did."

I paused, still staring out the window. "You would have jumped in, too?"

Momma reached for my hand. "You saved Alane, didn't you, Beauty? Did you even think twice?"

I shook my head.

"You take care of who you love," Momma said. "There's no question of needing to even things up. You don't have to think about Great-Granny Dorothy Lu Lu's dying like that again."

"All right," I said, even though I knew that memory wouldn't ever let go of me, not all the way.

She squeezed my hand with her warm fingers.

"Let's go visit Alane," she said, and the two of us got out of the car.

The Shrivers' front door swung open wide before we even got up the porch stairs. Mrs. Shriver stood there like she'd been waiting for us a long time. I gathered up my courage and marched toward her. And even though she'd been so mad, Mrs. Shriver swooped down on me and gave me a tight hug.

"Thank you, Beauty," she said into my hair. "Thank you for being Alane's friend. You gave my baby something wonderful. I was so afraid, I didn't want her to do anything. But she's had so much fun with you."

I hugged Mrs. Shriver back. "Yes, ma'am."

"Laney's waiting for you in the family room." Alane's mother couldn't resist one little warning. "She can't stay up long. It's not good for her. Come on in, Nina," Mrs. Shriver said to Momma. She grabbed Momma by the arm. "You and I can have a snack while the girls chat."

"Sounds terrific, Anna," Momma said.

Since when were they on a first-name basis? Who cared? I was going to see Alane again!

"This way, this way," Mrs. Shriver said.

I followed her through the house. Everything was new and fancy, nothing like our home with all its old furniture and ancient family photos.

"I have to apologize for my husband. He has an early commitment in the morning and has gone on to bed." Mrs. Shriver led me into the den. "Now, Beauty, here's Alane. Would you like a brownie with ice cream?"

"Sure," I said. "Thank you."

Alane grinned at me from her La-Z-Boy recliner. "Me, too, Mom?" Her voice came out airy and light, like maybe she had taken in too big a breath.

"Okay, baby."

Momma and Mrs. Shriver left the room together.

"My momma calls me baby, too," I said. A thought of Mrs. Shriver without Alane popped into my head. What would a momma do without her daughter? The idea was just awful. I shook that picture out of my head and moved to a chair near my friend. "Are you feeling all right?"

"Of course," Alane said. "Don't I look like it?"

She had a new wig, that same dark color as the one before, but shorter this time. Still, she *didn't* look all right. She looked worn out. There were dark circles under her eyes. And she seemed even older somehow, like the hospital had stolen years from her. Or maybe the river had.

"I think you look great." It was the truth. I was so glad to see her again.

Alane grabbed my hand and tilted her head toward me. She looked over my shoulder to make sure our moms were gone, then whispered, "Did you see her, too, Beauty?"

"Who?"

"Great-Granny Dorothy Lu Lu."

I shook my head. "No, Alane," I said. "I didn't."

"Are you sure?" Alane sat back in the chair and closed her eyes. "Can you believe it? She came after all. I *saw* her."

Overhead, a ceiling fan swirled with a soft *thwi, thwi, thwi* sound. I could hear Momma's and Mrs. Shriver's murmured voices in the other room. Were they talking about Alane?

"I'm glad you had a chance to meet her," I said.

"She was just beautiful, all that long blond hair, like in the picture at your house." Alane's eyes gleamed. She smiled big.

"She seemed so nice. Like she was there to make sure we got out of the water."

"Really?"

Alane nodded. "I'm not so scared about dying now." She shook her head. "Your great-grandmother was just so calm. She let me know that she'd be waiting for me. That I didn't have to be afraid."

"She'll be there waiting for you?" Goosebumps covered my arms and legs.

"That's what she told me. That people who love us are waiting for us on the other side."

I thought for a moment of my memory of that day so long ago. Again, I could hear the frantic calls of my family, could almost feel the cold water and Great-Granny Dorothy Lu Lu's hands clinging to me.

"Listen, Beauty. I need your help." Alane's words pulled me back.

"What?"

"It's a big favor."

"I'll do it," I said. "You know I will, Alane."

She cleared her throat. I could hear our mothers' voices getting louder, coming closer. "Remember that book I said I wanted to write?" she asked. "At the beginning of school, when we talked about what we wanted to be when we grew up?"

The beginning of school seemed like ages ago.

"I remember."

"Well, I can't do it alone. It's just too hard. But I want to get it done. I *have* to get it done. And there's not a lot of time left for me to do it."

Don't say that, I thought. "I'll do it," I said. "Whatever it is."

"Wait. You don't even know what I'm going to say." Alane squeezed my hands.

"It doesn't matter," I said. "I'll help you write your book. I'll be your scribe if you want. I'll do whatever you think I should."

"Even put in a song or two?"

"An 'On Top of Old Smoky' song?"

Alane laughed. "Yes. I want this to be a book that we do. Together. We'll tell all. The fun times, the sad times, even the Great-Granny Dorothy Lu Lu things. What do you think?"

I couldn't help but grin.

"I've even got a title for it," Alane said. "It came to me on the river."

Then Mrs. Shriver and Momma burst into the family room, holding plates full of ice cream and brownies.

Alane giggled. "*Pretty Like Us,*" she whispered. "Meaning you and me. That's the title."

"The title for what?" Momma asked. She handed me a plate and spoon, then sat on the sofa across from Alane and me.

I looked at my friend. "Oh, nothing," I said to Momma.

Pretty Like us.

It just might work.

CAROL LYNCH WILLIAMS is the author of more than twenty books for young readers. Raised in Florida, she did borrow her mother's car many times but never ran into a boar—though she did squish an armadillo once. She still feels horrible about that. Carol, the mother of seven children, lives in Utah.